AND HE DECIDED TO LIVE

MAGIC HAPPENS WHEN YOU START TO LIVE

Satyapriya Badatya

INDIA • SINGAPORE • MALAYSIA

ISBN 979-8-89588-338-9

Acknowledgments

I will begin by offering my sincere gratitude to my parents Mr. Trilochan Badatya and Mrs. Jayanti Badatya for being the loveliest couple and always stand by my side. I have no words to show my thankfulness to them. My sister Laki Badatya who always stand by my side and encourage me to pursue my passion for writing, thank you for always there for me. My uncles Mr. Banabas Badatya, Mr. Bhaskar Badatya and Mr. Prasanta Badatya thank you for your guidance, without your help I wouldn't be here. My jiju Mr. Promod Badatya and my nephew Ansh and Bansh thank you for coming our life.

I would like to dedicate this book to my late friend Jagannath Gouda. I will always be great full for your love and support. Our memories will always with me till the end. Our friendship is incomplete without the name Chitrasen Pradhan. Thank you Chitra for being most memorable part of my life. Thank you for everything, thank you for your presence.

Special thanks to my friend Divya Panday and Arjoma Chattopadhyay for your help and guidance throughout my writing journey. Thank you for your time, thank you for being there when no one is there, always being a wonderful company and giving a fresh perspective.

There is no need to thank you guys because in the end we all are one. Thank you Saraj Kumar Behera and Subham Patel for being the best roommate ever. Literally I have no words to show my love to you guys. Thank you for listening those 3am stupid thoughts. Thank you for your believe in me.

In this stage of life, we always need a guidance, I would like to thank you my two elder Brother Biswajit Swain and Abinash

Mohanty. Thank you for treating me like your younger brother and your friendly guidance will always encourage in life.

I would like to thank you each one of you who is holding this book right now in your hand. Thankyou for choosing this one. If this could change a decimal in your life then it will be my best reward.

Last but not the least I will show my gratitude to my publisher for all your hard work to change my dream into reality, thankyou for being ever supportive. Team notion press.

———

'Soldiers!!

Let's start today's Royal Justice process', King said.

not again…

Just ignore him,

J&J I can hear you, as I can see you have no fear to your king,

King?

Which King comes to Royal Court without shoes? where is your Royal Shoes?

Shut up …. you tiny squirrel twin,

How dare you to talk like that, to your King.

'Is breakfast ready'? pooh asked,

Not yet son, I will wake you up when it's ready.

'You can take rest now,' King said

Why are you love him so much?

'God knows what he is doing here, leaving north pole', J murmured

'Where is Pony and Gugu?', King asked

Oh, here they are coming,

You have a complaint, right Pony?

Tell us what is it.

'Someone had stolen my carrot from my room', Pony said

'Oh, no, this is a very serious matter, we have to find out soon', King said

'I am telling you; he must have stolen', J&J said

'Will you please lock your mouth for a sec.', king said to J.

Yes Pony, tell us every detail, when was the last time, you saw your carrot?

'Yesterday night. I ate half of it and saved the other half for today's breakfast', Pony said

You can't even finish a full carrot; then why do you bring such big carrots?

Have you brushed? king asked

No, which rabbit brush his teeth? and J&J also don't brush their teeth.

'They are kids', King said

'I am telling you, he has stolen the carrot', J said.

Yes, 'I saw him, he was heading towards Pony's room last night', J said

'J&J, why are you making fun of me and blaming me always', pooh said angrily

If you guys speak a single word against me, I will sit on you.

And what do you think, we will keep quiet, we will break your jaws, (J&J said together)

(King laughed...)

What are you saying J&J, hardly you will be six hundred grams when you both combined and pooh is alone more than a quintal.

Tell him to keep quite or we will send him back to north pole.

'This is my home', pooh said sadly,

Home, the weight you are carrying you need a godown not home, you fat white panda.

(everybody starts to laugh)

J&J again called me fat, pooh complained,

'Are you guys done? Breakfast is ready', Gugu said.

'J&J, Pony, learn something from Gugu how discipline she is', King said

And pooh?

He is new here, give him some time

Coming Gugu, in a minute.

Pony? last week you had same complaint about lost carrot, right? Then I brought another one for you and later we find out that, it was not stolen but you were hidden it somewhere safe so that you can get another one. Is it the same mistake you are repeating?

'Pony, look at me', King said,

(There was complete silence)

This silence means you are guilty and you should be punished.

According to memory land Article Five, your punishment is you will be tickled for one minute nonstop.

King lifted Pony for tickling, then suddenly there is light everywhere, and there is a sound, like when you are in sleep and someone trying to wake you up and it is getting clear and louder in every second.

Mr. B A R H A D...

Mr. B A R H A D...

Mr. Barhad,

Please keep that saline bottle at its place,

(Kamala Didi said while sliding the curtains of the window)

What Kamala Di, why you disturbed at this moment, Gugu prepared a delicious Breakfast, we were about to eat.

Really, what was she prepared?

I don't know, you wake me up before I saw,

(Kamala Di laughed)

'Good morning, Sam', Lakshya said

'Kamala Di, you also know about his dream', Lakshya asked curiously

This is his third time here in hospital in twenty days, this much I know, it's obvious.

'Have you given him something to eat?', Lakshya asked,

'Is he still there? he came here by following your Ambulance. Last night I gave him bread and left over foods', Kamala di said

He would have here near the bed, If Hospitals will allow street dogs, right Kamala di?

Absolutely, if it was a cute Labrador or a Pomeranian, then definitely he would have here.

'Street dogs are not allowed to anywhere', - Kamala di said

Humans are strange. We are the only species in the universe who discriminate so much. He was born in road side then what is his fault with this? The best thing about animals are they don't Judge or calculate you before they love you like we humans do or there would have no love for Humans, Lakshya said

I am going to give him something to eat.

How is lily, kamala di? how her study going on?

She in tenth. she was saying something about ET IT something like that,

IIT?

Yes, IIT. She will do coaching for that from next year.

My husband lost all our saving in property dealing. He gave all our money to a broker and later we got to know that all the documents and papers are fake, that land was also already someone else's name. He filled a complaint against him in police station, it's been two months. Still there is no result.

He has only few years to retire. Lily's coaching fees, home expenses, all the medical expenses, we are spending all our salary on it. There is no saving for future.

Don't worry Kamala di everything will be fine.

Hey, look here guys, who is with me', Lakshya said

Ravi babu, Kamala di said

God morning, Guys,

Mummy made paratha for breakfast, here take it.

'Outside food is not allowed here', Kamala di said

Footsteps are approaching,

Maybe doctor is coming, hide all this, quick.

'How are you doing Mr. Barhad?', Dr. said

I checked all your reports, everything is under control but you have to take care of yourself. As a human we have to work entire life but if we can't take care of our body then there is no mean of our hard work, don't take stress too much.

Yes doctor,

May I go to home now doctor?

Take rest for now, you could go in one or two hours.

Thank you doctor.

'Now open the box I am starving', Ravi said

Paratha and okra potato dry mix,

'Kamila di please sit, Let's have Breakfast together', Lakhya said

Sure, his mother knows me very well, we both are from Same village though she is elder than me. But not today, I have to clean this ward and other two wards, there is lot of work today.

(Kamila di left)

'Where is curd and pickle? these two things go very well with parathas', Ravi said

'Actually, mama is allergic to curd, so she always make something to replace curd', Sam said

Do you guys know how paratha got famous in India? Ravi asked

In Mughal periods, there was a place called Firangi Mahal in Lucknow. There was a tree in that place and a small hotel was there under that tree, where soldiers, travelers, passengers and tourists used to eat there. That time Halwa-puri was famous but the owner of that hotel wasn't very good in making Puris.

One day when everything was finished, almost every single item, Suddenly, two passengers came and there was only two tandoori Rotis left. The passengers requested to please bring whatever he has; they are dying out of hunger. Then the cook of that hotel did one thing, he covered ghee both side of the roti and heated it in a pan or tawa. That hard roti became soft and tasty. These two passengers loved it and every time they came, they ordered same ghee tandoori Roti. With time it became paratha and then people start to add stuffing inside it. Now there are more than hundreds of stuffing parathas are there, somehow Butter chicken also has the same story.

Would you guys listen?

Please No,

(They both said together)

There also a Paranthe Wali Gali in Delhi.

'And now you are here in Bhubaneswar stop your Imagination it getting cold, let's just eat first', Sam said

No matter how many items you make but paratha with Pickle, combination made in heaven.

Aunty could have made another dish by using Curd and Okra it's called "Dahi Bhindi" it is very famous in north.

'You guys wants to know the recipe', Ravi asked

 NO,

(Lakshya and Sam Said it loudly).

'Since you guys' Insist me so much, please listen carefully', Ravi Said.

Heat some oil in a pan then add roughly cut onion, ginger, garlic in it after they got soft and onion become translucent, take it to a mixer and make a paste after it comes to room temperature. In the same pan add some more Oil add long cut okras, lite fry them till they become dark green after that keep these Okras aside.

Now on same pan add some more oil wait till heat. then add mustard, cumin, fenugreeks and asafetida and add curry leaves also after they heat completely add that paste which you prepared before. Cook for some time then add - turmeric, chili powder and coriander powder with salt. Now cook this paste till oil starts to separate, you can add some water If you want. after that slow the flame and add whipped curd on it, remember masalas should be cooked properly before you add curd and flame should be low if not, then the curd will curdle.

Now add the fried okras on to it, cook for five minutes then at last add coriander leaves and garam masala and your "Dahi Bhindi" recipe is ready.

I learned it from my mom.

I still don't know whom I love the must to eat or to cook, I love them both, to be honest, l am alive only to eat.

(everybody Laughed)

'Whatever you say no one can beat auntie's paratha', Ravi said

'Wow cook himself praised', Sam said

Not cook, Say Chef,

'There is a different between Cook and Chef', Ravi said

What difference? They Both prepare food for others.

Nah, every Chef is a cook but every cook can't be a Chef. Anyone who makes food can be cook like persons who makes food in marriages or who runs a small Hotel in road side or who make food in Dhaba's.

But chef is different, He makes food, along with he represents a sense of style, Luxury and Culture with food. Chefs generally works at 5-star hotels. Ships, travel with diplomates and Businessman.

And to became a chef I have to study culinary Arts.

what is this? Sam asked

In culinary arts they train you how to become chef. Including cooking, preparation, presentation of food, proper Garnishing and Customer service.

'Okay, do whatever you want but before finish your law First', Sam said

Actually, I have decided not to continue law further.

What?

(Both said at same time with a piece of paratha in their mouth)

you can't Just leave in middle of semester.

Law was never my first choice, my father forced so, I had to take it, but now it feels like l am done with it.

'Are you out of your mind, what are you saying, you can't leave it like that, it's just one year, please wait till then. After that do whatever you want to do', Sam said

Lakshya, please say something to him.

I think he is right - Lakshya said,

Look Ravi it doesn't matter whether you study law or culinary arts it must be your decision, only yours, today you leaving law for the chef thing, it should not happen that tomorrow you leave that for something else.

Whatever you want do, do it with your full heart and take responsibility for that, doesn't matter if you get success or failure but there should be your one hundred percent involvement. Most of us are in a race where we don't know to where we are heading. I am happy that you are choosing your own race.

No one knows what tomorrow will bring, but we have present in our hand. If we have a best today then definitely there will be a better tomorrow.

'Come back to reality guys, this dialogs only works in movies. In our society there is a system and we all have to go through it', Sam said

How are you going convince your father?

'My sister and mom will take care of it, you guys don't worry', Ravi said

I got to go now.

Me also, getting late for my class.

(Both left)

Again, that silence, again that loneliness, it's like this emptiness trying to kill me every second. Not a single hope from anyone. The silence which is buried inside me trying to scream but who will listen? who will understand? Sometimes it feels like I born for this loneliness. Does silence have any sound? whom am I asking this, who will give the answer to me? Whenever I look Inside, I find myself in chain in my leg, that chain made from some questions. That chain is so heavy that no answer can break it, the more I try to escape, the more I got trapped in it, with time the questions became deeper and the chain become heavier and there is no hope for any answer.

(What are you thinking? - Gugu asked

Why me? why he made me like this, what was my fault and for how long I have to fight with myself, Then against the society. Every single day I am fighting two battles, one with myself and one with society. Every day I gear up by taking a sword of fake hope, but I have no Idea for which side l am fighting. Even If I win, what will I get and after losing everyday why this battle is still going on.

Sam said all these in a breath with full of tears in his eyes,

'I don't understand why you humans have such problem, you are dealing with problem really well, but the moment someone asks 'Is everything ok'? then you guys start crying, strange.' Gugu said.

God has given everything to humans. you are different from everything in this world but you know the sad part is you have problem with each other, you guys can't live peacefully with each other.

God... who told him to make me like this. He gave everything to everyone except me. It would have best that he never created me. If he will meet me one day then I will ask him. You know the irony is I have to die to ask him. I have to take help of death to meet him. He is very cleaver, He left me here to die every day, even if I get a chance to get my answer after a real death, what will I do with that answer, there is nothing to prove to anyone because at that moment my existence is gone with my question and pain.

Sometimes I feel like I Scream to the world and tell them,

'Yes, l am a gay', I like boys and l am different from all of you.

No god cursed me, I don't have any mental issue I don't have to go to any exorcist or Sorceress for my treatment neither I have to take medicine for that.

Why this love thing is so simple and yet complicated, why love mean, one boy and one girl always comes to our mind. If love has no boundaries and it is beyond of anything then why our love is categorized?

I don't know why people sees us in a disgusting way specifically here, where they exactly know what this thing is, still they hate us so much. But they never tried to understand why they hate us so much.

And our beloved god is also not far away behind that, if he created a man first then why he created a woman to company him. He could have created a man also in the garden of Eden. I know for a certain biological process and to create next generation men and women both we need but all this concept came after eaten the fruit from forbidden tree, my question to God is why didn't he created another men to give company to first created man, another question is if creation of next generation was only purpose, then why he gave emotions to human like love, hate, joyfulness, jealousy. There would have no love no kindness no hate for other. Man, women come closer, they mate and there will be next generation. Sometimes I wonder how it will be a world with emotionless humans, will it be a better world or a worse one? I think there will be a better world without emotions.

'Yes, there will be no love for others. no kindness for others, no care for others, no friendship with others, what are you sayings?', Gugu reacted.

Emotions are sweetest thing in this world. Because of emotion you are a human or there will be no difference between a human and animal.

Why God not categorized animal in this category. Have you ever seen two male tigers making love with each other or be with each other. If this world is perfect then why l am not part of this world, why l am different in the crowd, again question is the same, who's fault is this, is it God? evolution process? science or genetics? I don't know who is responsible for that but I am suffering.

Everything will be alright

'How is Amit', Gugu asked

He is good, as I am here, he is handling whole business out there. He is talented, handling clients really well. He is just 27 but at this age the way he is taking care of everything really appreciable. He is calm, the way he listens every problem acts according and delivers best solution always and obviously he is handsome, perfectly trimmed beard, brown eyes with shine hair enough to attract anyone. He never misses the Gym. Most important thing is he has a kind heart, listens to everyone and respects everyone's feeling.

Few days back there was an accident on the road and Amit was passing by, he called the Ambulance and send them to Hospital.

(Gugu cleared his throat and said,)

It seems like someone going to fall in love very soon. By the way anyone could have done the Same what Amit did, you Just praising him more.

Gugu said and laughed.

Yes, I like him, He is cute and sweet, it would be the best if we were together but this will not happen, we can't and we shouldn't change anyone for our happiness neither we should force someone to love us. I Just always want to see him Happy around me. Seeing him Happy and with his smile I forget my pain for a while.

But I don't want to forget that thing happened fifteen years back, I don't want to go through same thing again. I don't want to go through the same pain again. If it comes back to me at this stage, I don't know if I *could handle this or not. If I had a time machine, I would never have allowed that thing happen to me, could have changed everything.*

'Yes, but whatever we are today because of our past. If those things never happened to us, we would never be here, whatever our past is, it's good or bad it's our, we can't change it and we shouldn't even try to change it', Gugu said

Sam brings a smile in his face and said,

My past was bad and my present is worse, so I don't in favor of changing things. Both way there is suffering for me. I still think about that how and why he did that to me. I never told them that I want to play with them I only Joined them Because he told me to Join, my only fault was that I was in love with him.)

(Knock... knock... sound came from the door)

('Someone is coming, typical humans they don't even allow to cry someone peacefully', Gugu said)

'Are you crying Sam, what happened? let me call the doctor', Kamala di said.

No, no, Didi it's fine. You should have at your home at the time, you still here, Is everything ok?

'I hope l am not disturbing you', Kamala di Said

 No, please tell.

Actually, my elder sister has a daughter and they are looking for a right man for marriage. Our Aradhya is very hardworking, very good at study she got a job in a bank last month and she is very beautiful.

What is in my mind is Lakshya and Ravi both are very sweet and I know them well, if you could talk to them for me as I can't talk to them directly about this.

Oh, I thought it was for me, am I not good enough for your Aradhya? (Sam said, and laughed)

Just kidding didi, please don't mind…

To be honest kamala di, these things are not very common today anymore. At your time there was a mediator who search for a boy or girl and connects two families. then there is some astro talk, if everything goes well then direct marriage, In between there is no talk and no meet up between the boy and girl. It was enough if you have a photo of him or her.

Kids now a days focus on their career and future more. everyone has their Individual goals and aims; everyone wants to be Independent and everyone loves their freedom too and more than that how to co-operate with each other, emotional bonding, financial discussions, future planning, work life balance, saving, everything depends before marriage.

This is only one part, in other love, live in, one side love, get over from Exs, mature understanding, these discussions also matters before marriage. Then after they think about marriage. It's not like everyone think about it but. Most of the kids think about all these before marriage.

'Now it feels like we had the best time', Di said

Maybe, but with time there is change in society and according that peoples also change. Here no one is right or wrong, everyone takes decisions as their benefit.

Ravi is two year is younger them me and Lakshya. He is now twenty-six we both had same school, Lakhya's school was different. His father in a transport business and mother is a home maker and she has a YouTube Channel, where she shows, some art and crafts and Ravi's sister Reena is doing architect. They Just moved to Bhubaneswar seven years back. Before that they were same village as mine. His grandparents still live there and his grandmother has health Issues. Though Malti Didi is there to take care of them, she cooks for them, clean the house and do all other works. Actually, her husband is in other city for work and she has a boy about eight, nine years, after sending her son to school and finishing her own work she goes there. She loves to spend time with Ravi's grandparents. Though Ravi's father gives some money to Malti di every month. She never accepts that, then he started to send it directly to her bank account.

Ravi's father requested so much to his parents to shift Bhubaneswar with them. But Ravi's grandfather clearly says no to them, he says he put all his hard work to build this home he just can't leave it, it's not Just a home, for him it's a family member. Except that he loves the calm healthy environment of village as compared to Bhubaneswar's pollution.

Ravi's grandmother is so sweet, sometimes they both visits here but not more than two days. In every two, three months Ravis family visit village and other time they talk over phone. Now a days they visit less to village as the business is growing so uncle don't get enough time and it will affect Ravi and Reena's study and you know Ravi very well...

As he says. He is only alive to eat. He was gollu mollu when he was a kid. when we wear in school there was mid-day meal system by Govts. The women who used to cook for us, Ravi was always with her and helped her with cooking. whenever there was food there was Ravi. Most of the time we found him in our School-kitchen not classroom and all our teaches well aware about that but since his love for food and his cute face always saved him from any punishment.

You wouldn't believe Kamala Di, our friendship also began with food. that time I was in sixth and Ravi was at fourth standard. That day when our school about to close, heavy rain came with massive clouds. We all waited for the rain to stop so that we can go home, we waited almost one hours but there is no sign of rain to stop. Most of us didn't have umbrellas, some kids had but they are also waited for the wind to slow down. After some time, everybody's parents came to take their child with them. Ravi didn't have an umbrella and Reena was in leave that day. I also didn't have an umbrella. But I had a big plastic polythene. In a triangular shape so that it could work like a temporary raincoat, my mother used to keep it in my bag even If I force her to not to keep it that time, when we couldn't even afford an umbrella.

Every student now gone there were only me, Ravi and two of our teachers. They were also waiting for us to go then they can lock it. Rain became slow a bit and them I unfold my polythene to go, then don't know why I looked at Ravi, He was already looking at me with full of tears in his eyes it's like If I say a single word to him, he will start crying. He came to me and said with very slow and adorably "bhaya I am feeling hungry", imagine that situation, there is no sign of rain to stop, everybody is gone and only thing in his mind was 'food'. That moment we talked for the very first time then I asked Ravi Is there anyone from your home coming? and he said my father is out of town for his business work. Then I fold the polythene to make is like rectangle so that we both are at least cover our head from rain. We both stuck our plastic polythene bag that we used to carry our books to school, that time bag packs were so expensive only few could afford that. We both stuck our plastic bag in between our arms, cover our head with plastic and ran towards home before we reach my left side and his right-side wear completely wet. Ravi's home was a bit for from my home so we reached our home, my mama was waiting for me. We clean ourself and by the time Mama served food for both of us without saying anything, mother knows everything I still remember there was "palak Ke Ghate" mama prepared that day.

'What is that? I am listening the name for very first time', Kamala di asked.

It was an old traditional village food as more likely a desi Soup, I don't have an exact recipe of it, Ravi can explain these things really well.

As far I know for that we need spinach leaves, Rice and some lentil. The preparation process is very simple and Plain, we don't need any turmeric or chilly for that and it is really healthy.

Roast the rice and lentil in low heat then add some water and let it cook, after a ninety percent cook add Spanish to it now cook until it's done. In last for the seasoning, heat oil, add some chopped onion garlic with mustard seeds, you can add dry chills If you want. Now your "palak Ke Ghate" is ready.

This is the exact process, I guess. You can eat it with rice or eat it as Stew from that it is one of Ravi favorite dish, from that day we are friends.

'Lakshya is calmer and more decent, isn't he?', Kamala di said

Exactly di, Sam replied

He is different from us. He is a great son, perfect student and more than that he is a good human. He never fights with anyone, never talk loud to anyone. Best in studying, state level tennis player. Always wear a Navy-blue Jeans and light blue full sleeve shirts with folded sleeves until it's not a special occasion. Well maintained body, trimmed beard with a fragrance of mild perfume and a watch which was gifted by his math teacher when he was in twelfth. He has a personality and he know how to carry himself. It's like, whatever you are searching inside a perfect groom it's inside Lakshya.

He was very clear about his studying; He wants to became a psychologist. He is very sure about that. In these matters he is like Tendulkar in cricket.

'Psycho... what? what is this, it must have required lot of money and have to go abroad to study, and what will be the salary once he gets a job it must be in lakhs', Kamala di asked curiously.

Yes Didi, it depends, psychologist means the person who helps to come over mental disease, you have marked in ward no. 13. There is a person comes once in a week for two three hours and there were also four five patients. They talk about their problems and the work of psychologist is to solve this with therapy. Psychologist are different from doctors, as they don't do any operation or surgeries, they only give therapies.

Lakshya was very clear about his career since school. He was different from any normal students in many ways. he used to read sci-fi comic books where we had no idea what it was, along with school book, he used to read other books also, it's not like he is a bookworm, He Just loves to read, along with he is very good at cricket and volleyball but it's difficult to beat him in tennis.

Lakshya's parents Runs a network of private schools. You can say that in every city there is school and their head office here in Bhubaneswar. They manage everything from here. They never put any kind of pressure on Lakshya neither in field of study or sports. One thing to learn here is how beautiful Lakshya's parents' mange both personal and professional life. His grandfather is a retired economic professor. Till now he spent lot of his time in reading. He is now writing a book; I don't know the title but it's something about rural economic growth. His grandmother passed away when he was seventeen. Whenever I go to his home. I talk a lot with his grandfather, there is a lot to learn from him. In fact, he helped me so much in growth of my business.

His family financially very strong that even if Lakhya don't do anything still then they can pass two generations easily. They could have made anything to Lakshya like doctor or engineer or economist but they allow him to make his own decision apart from money. The upbringing and the teaching they given to Lakshya there is no comparison you will never see him in anger. He is always calm, humble and down to earth with a smile in his face.

Lakshya and me had same class but never been in same school. His family also used to live the same village as our but after his grandmother's death they shifted to Bhubaneswar. In our village there was only one two-stair building, where they used to live. They had very first television in our village and very first landline phone also. That time we all get to know how rich kids look like. when we saw Lakshya. Complete clean well folder and ironed school uniforms, he had different dresses for different things like for school, for regular use, for sports and for night. I used to go his house for watching tv. I love to see things which normal people can't see like how rich people talk with each other, how they place things how they behave in their home there is always a sweet small from their home. my favorite channel was animal plants in his home.

That was the complete details of my two friends, now you decide who is the best for your Aradhya, but I don't think they will agree for marriage right now. If you could wait three four years and something could happen.

'No doubt Lakshya is the best', Kamala Di said.

May I ask you something, if you don't mind.

Yes Didi of course.

You are such a big businessman, everyone in the city knows you very well, every minister, all movie stars form Odisha knows you personally. You are such an inspiration among youths. Big house, properties, luxury cars all you have and I will pray to God that, it will grow everyday but no one seen your father with you and no one knows about your father there is only your mother with you always.

('What is wrong with these humans, why they scratch the wounds every time', Gugu whispered

I don't know may be the more we try to avoid our fear, the more it will come to us till we face it. I don't want to talk about this to anyone.)

Sam... Sam...

'I am sorry if I asked something wrong, I shouldn't have asked that', Kamala Di said,

It's not like that Didi

(Suddenly door knocks)

Raghu?

'Please come', Sam said.

Amit sir told me to take you home, he already talked with doctor and we can go now.

Didi meet Raghu. He works in our office. Very hard-working sincere guy.

Give me 2 mins then we will go.

(Raghu saved me by coming at right time.

or Amit saved you by sending Raghu at right time - Gugu said and laughed)

'Let's go Raghu, take me to office first', Sam said

No sir Amit sir's clear instruction to take you to home, mama is waiting for you.

Okay Let's go to Anna's we have to take Mama's favorite Dosa, then sector 13 for Srikhand, they make Best Srikhand in Bhubaneswar. I know she must not have eaten at last night since I was in hospital.

'Have you done breakfast Raghu? ', Sam asked.

Yes, sir I already have.

Still, you will eat with us.

Thank you, sir, but lam full today, may be another day.

'Mummy, please come fast, 1 am starving, food is here what are you doing in kitchen', - Sam said

How is your leg? Swelling is still there, next week we are going to Delhi, I have taken the appointment for Dr. Shrivastava.

I am fine, no need to go anywhere.

How were parathas, it must be cold by the time Lakshya reaches there.

Yes, it was not that warm.

Ravi was saying who sends Okra Potato dry mix with paratha, and guess what, he ate most of it.

I know - (Mummy laughed)

I should have packed more.

No, mama it was sufficient for all, Kamala Di also ate from it.

Where is Mamta Didi,

Her son wasn't feeling well so she was saying for one day leave, I gave her two.

That means all the house works and parathas are done by you. There was no one to help. Mama why are you doing this. How many times I have to tell you, please don't do all these, it's putting extra pressure on your leg don't you remember what doctor said last time. I could have arranged someone else, and Mamta di taking too much leave now a days as you are not saying anything to her.

It's not like that, she is very good in heart.

In every week there is new oil packet in grocery list. where does these oils are going, we only two people eat still a new pocket is being used in every week, I think we are drinking oil, right Mama?

Calm down Simu, whatever she needs taking from our kitchen I know that, it's just that she is not taking permission before that.

It's called theft Mama.

Whatever, we wear also in same situation one day.

yes, but we never steal anything from anyone. Many nights we slept with empty stomach but we never tried to snatch others food.

Mr. Dash was called, why did you choose Kolkata for new factory? that place is not feel safe to me.

For the expansion of our business that is a best place.

In last six months the sell on that region on the top as compared to western region of Odisha to save all the transport expenses and taxes we need to open a factory there. I know this will be not easy from taking permission from govt. to land acquisition to start production it will take very long time so we need help from Mr. Dash.

Do whatever you think is right l am with you, but remember one thing, expand business, luxury, leaving a legacy it's all good, but Inner Joyfulness, self- satisfaction and a blissful life, no money can buy that.

Yes, Mama I know that, but we have to fulfill the demand.

Don't get me wrong Simu, l am Just saying whatever we have today it's enough, I know what not you have done to build this Empire, I don't need a single thing from that all I need is you, I always want to see you happy and smiley, I just want you to come back home before sunset everyday that's it.

Don't worry Mama I will be fine; give your plate I will wash them.

Gupta ji was saying there is girl in his relative I think you should meet her once.

Not again mama, I have already told you I don't want to get married now and why Gupta ji is so concern about my marriage, why don't he focus on his blood pressure and asthma.

Ok don't marry l am already last stage of my life. I thought I would spend rest of my life playing with my grandchild but since you are denying for marriage, I will die with my dream. Today or tomorrow, everyone has to go.

Mama I am telling you, it's enough, stop the emotional drama. I am not saying I am not going to marry; I am Just saying I need some time.

I will do it whenever I feel that I am ready for marriage, you also got married, we both know what happened after that and you are not going anywhere.

Alright since you are so grown up that you can make your own decision, I don't think you need me anymore.

Okay I will do whatever you want (Sam said in frustration) but I have a condition, I need some time, call Gupta ji for address I will meet her. Then I will decide.

Here, take this.

What have you done to your body, you look like a prisoner why this long beard, get yourself clean then meet her.

What! you already have the address, now I know, this is the reason for this whole drama.

Mama smiled and said "yes"

(Next day in office)

'Raghu where is Amit', Sam asked

He is in the field- Raghu replied

Why?

Again, the main electric line disconnected from the substation. last night there was heavy rain and massive wind speed is responsible for that. He was saying in last three months it is second time. He is with electric department to fix this thing permanently.

'Why didn't you call me', Sam asked

He said not to Include you, as he can handle this small thing alone. -Raghu replied

Sir, Reema and her friends waiting for you.

'Hello Sam, how are you doing now? I thought you are in home so I called you there but Mama said, you already left for office and here we are to give you extra stress', Reema said

(everybody laughed)

'How you guys doing? Somesh, Lalit, Ridhi', Sam asked

We are good sir.

Don't call me Sir. Just Sam,

'All the legal documentation process about to finish from Animal welfare board. Now it's time we should work like as organize manner. All the guidelines, acts, sections and legal paper works. Ridhi is handling all those things. Lalit, sorry Dr. Lalit has a clinic still he will be working with us. Somesh will handle our social media and IT related work and I will manage the all things including fund', Reema said.

I still remember this, how we stated all this. about two and half year ago. That time we didn't have any vehicle, any shelter nor any funding to help those innocence souls. Sam, you remember Lata's story, that pregnant cow, who was hit by a car, when local people called us. That time we didn't have any customize vehicle and it was raining, so you me and Somesh we went there to help her in a scooty. She was really in pain and was struggling for life by the time we reach there and we didn't have any experience, it was our first call without further delay I called Dr. Subash. He was a great veterinarian at that time, I gave him every detail, then he said bring her to hospital, it is only way to save her. It was a difficult Job to do with the rain. Somesh and Sam went to arrange a vehicle so that we can take her to hospital after few minutes a driver agreed to take her but he charged double. Now the problem was we three can't lift a pregnant cow to a mini truck, we must need some help but due to the rain no one came, then we give them some money and some locals helped us. We Immediately took her to hospital and Dr. Subash started his work by the time her condition was really bad.

Then suddenly something magical happened where we all are about to give up. Dr. Subash not only saved Lata but also Lata gave birth a baby-Lata, right that moment we give her a name, it's Rani which mean princess. It was Just the god's plan or a mother's love to bring her child to this world no one knows. We were so happy that everyone started to cry.

I still remember what Dr. Subash said, you guys not only saved two lives but also you saved the humanity. The world is full of such people who hit her.

Oh, those moments when you do something for others selflessly, it hits differently, what I am saying is beginning is always hard but by time we learn everything, always remember our motto

"No hunger - No pain". For that whatever we could do, we will do.

'So, what is the plan', Sam asked,

To be an organization whether it is a government or not, we need certain certification and documentation. Good news is in next four five days everything will be ready. then we can act in large scales and more legal ways and most importantly we can tackle the trust issues. In social medias we can promote ourself more openly that will definitely help us in funding.

Lalit? anything from you Sam asked.

Whatever we have for the treatment is very limited.

Most of the time we are doing treatment in tents. the problem is if the treatment goes long and by changing weather, we definitely need a permanent shelter so that we can do treatment more accurately and effectively. All our Important Medicine or treatment equipment can be stored there also we need a customize treatment vehicle or Animal Ambulance so that we can avoid situations like Lata faced. We can give our volunteers a basic medical training so that then act in emergencies till help comes.

'That's a good idea Lalit', Sam said

Somesh what is your plan?

We will continue this as we are doing but in large scale, we are doing well in online in YouTube, we are about to achieve one fifty thousand subscribers. In Facebook and Instagram, we have one hundred thousand follower's and we are first of our kind to reach fastest hundred thousand followers. Since people loves to see short videos, we upload everything including rescue mission to treatment or feeding videos to bring the awareness among people, we are very popular in social media specially among youths. In fact, whatever donation we received in last six months mostly from social media

So, the plan is we are going to hire someone who can manage our social media and promotion things more effectively because we don't have that much time to handle everything in one hand. We are going to put ads in social media to attracts donors.

In offline also we are getting popular but everyone has mobile people knows us more online. We are getting popular in mouth to mouth, as well as we will continue our posters, Banners and wall painting job. The moment we get permission from Animal welfare board then we start printing pocket size card. More likely visiting card. where one side there will be all our contacts and other side our QR code will be there, whoever wants to donate can donate directly through it. Sometimes people see our works and wants to donate but later change their mind but seeing QR Code In front to their eyes, it may change things into our favor.

And for the website everything is ready, the concept how it would look like, the domain and other technical thing will sort soon once registration is done. Our app is also will be ready after that more people could connect to us remotely. We are planning to bring a concept that whenever someone helps an animal by taking our help or individually, we highlight their name in our website and who saves more life and help more animal we declare them "Saviors of the Month" in our site but before that he or she should post selfies or videos on social media by tagging us. This could be more popular among teens and more than that they will know how it feels when they help others.

Last week something miracle happened, Mr. Jacob comment in our post "well done guys keep it up"

'Who is Mr. Jacob?', Ridhi asked.

He is a well-known, humanitarian. He has done lot of work in Africa regions, especially on girl's education, could you imagine someone leave his comfortable well deserving social life at the age of twenty-three only to help others. He worked in Uganda, Rwanda, Burundi like these nations for humanity. He was awarded by United Nations also. Recently one of his interviews went viral about "Why death is easy and being alive is hard". Please watch it once it will definitely change your perception for life. He is now just thirty-six. He sacrificed his complete adult-hood for humanity. Sometimes I feel like he is not human. It is too much for a human.

Last week there was an article in times of India about us that how we rescued and saved over one hundred and fifty animals in forty-five days, many International NGOs appreciated that thing, then posted this in our page where he gave his comment, may be in near future foreign funds also coming who knows. All this was possible only because of social media so we have to make it more organize and effective.

That's great Somesh you are doing a fantastic work, keep it going.

'Reema your turn now', Sam said.

So, now we have one permanent shelter which is very small and what Lalit suggested we will work on that. We have Lata, Rani and her child, five cows, two bullock, six dogs they all are physical disabled in our shelter and for them their care taker. Other two temporally shelters where three cows, four bullocks, four dogs and one cat is there. They all are under treatment we will release them after the treatment is over. so that there will be space for other animals. To be honest we want to keep them all but we cannot, we only keep those in our permanent shelter who can't live without support. For those temporary shelter which we made with help of locals, we are paying a rent to the owner of the land there is also two care takers working, a mini truck always in standby with the driver and a helper we are also paying for that including diesel. Apart from that medicines, foods, electric bills and other things that we are now paying for.

All the expanses that we are making including salary it's all coming from the man who is standing in front of. I don't know how much he is making from his business but I know the exact number, how much he spends to manage all this. He is doing it for last two and half years.

If I tell you last month figure exactly 91% of our expenses came from straight his pocket. 6% from offline donation ad 3% from online donation. total only nine percent come from donation and not only that the land we have our permanent shelter, also belongs to Him.

we have to promote ourself more for more funding so that we can Help more, we have to reach out to people, Somesh is doing very well through his vlogs and short videos. Question is why anyone will give his hard earn money to us, no one give their money to stranger. We have to make them believe that, you are not giving to us, it's you who are doing all this through your money, and make them promise that every single penny of their money will fulfill the purpose.

Once we get certified by animal welfare board. Definitely have more trust on us, we will focus on free source of marketing like social media, make more short videos which will connect their emotions, a good background music can do it easily.

For the paid Marketing on social media we have very small amount, whatever you want to, you can do in between that range,

'Noted', Somesh said

Funding will not come to us by walking we must generate the source and I have some Ideas, we can request to any public organization company for CSR fund. We can motivate people to adopt or we can convince them for virtual adaption, all they have to do is pay for the monthly expenses of a dog, they don't have to take them to home.

We will do crowd funding every month like 2-month back in Christmas we made Santa-dogs that was also viral, like that we could do something every month.

We can do collaboration with animal food production companies, that they can take them in their ads or can use our shelter to shoot, in return they give food to them.

We can contact to schools that they should allow their students to visit their shelter it will not generate any Income but it could definitely change their mind, and may in future they will also help to any innocent soul. Money is the only medium; our only purpose is somehow they will get help from anyone.

We are now operating in very small area, thanks to all temporary members who is doing their job without being paid. With funding we can definitely operate in bigger radius. We can spread it to other states also like Bihar and Jharkhand.

Talking about permanent shelter. I have an idea why can't we expand our old shelter; we can repair it as we need, it will save our time as compared to make a new one. After complete renovation we should name it as it is so close to our heart. A good name in my mind.

Say it - Ridhi said

It will be "Mohodadhi" which means ocean' in Odia, like the ocean has no ending our love for the animals also will never end.

'That's so sweet Reema', Sam said

You guys are doing relay a great Job, really putting your heart for it. Thank you so much guys for your effort to them.

'All these things are ok but what should be the name of our organization this is very important thing we are not talking about', Ridhi said

(everybody smiled)

Yes, according that I will design logo and all. Somesh said

'Sam, you pick a name, it is your dream that we all are living', Reema said

It's our dream now, to be honest I was also thinking about it, animals are express their happiness through their tails, how about "The Happie Tails"

'It sounds very adorable', Ridhi said everyone smiled, what could be a better name then this. "The Happie Tails"...

'Mama, why so less oil in this dish?', Sam asked sarcastically

It must have dropped from her by mistake.

'Days before there was no oil in kitchen, now its floating, who done this magic', Sam said and laughed.

Are you done, now eat no talking.

'So, when are you going?', Mama asked.

We are going, I have told you next week, all the arrangements done. Appointments taken.

I was talking about the girl.

Which girl? - Sam replied

The girl Gupta ji was...

You know what I am not talking about it anymore. As you so grown up, you can make your own decision, what can I say.

Mama... don't start the drama please. I am telling you, I will do Nagin dance in, Gupta ji's funeral.

What?

Nothing.

'I have Just one question what will he get by destroying someone's life. why he losing his reputation, tell him to don't Interfere in my personal life', Sam said

Are you going to meet her or not? - Mama asked angry

Mama, listen

Say Yes or No,

Yes, Mama, I promise you I will but not before next week. First, we meet doctor in Delhi, then I will.

(Gugu, Pooh, Pony, J&J where are you guys?

'We can't come, we got to finish a very Important work', J&J said

'Stop playing with each other's tail and come fast', Sam said

Which game we will play today? Pony asked

Is there something to eat - Pooh said

'Make it clear If you want to play that stupid king soldier game then we don't have any time for that', J&J said

'Is everything ok?', Gugu asked

'I don't know, the more I try to run from something, it feels like l am only getting closer to it', Sam said

What happened, Pony asked

Nothing, I just wanted to talk to you guys.

'ls he, ok? Why he looking so sad', Pooh said

'Mama Insisting me to marry and this time it feels like there is no choices left for me', Sam said with a sad voice.

'Then do it, if she is beautiful then what is the problem. Anyway you are getting Old', J&J said

'J&J I am serious, I can't do it, you guys know that. I have already a spoiled life, I can't let another one spoil by me for your information l am twenty-eight only', Sam said.

Mama is forcing me to meet her,

'Then meet her and say that you don't want to get married', Pony said

It's not that easy Pony, mama has two three proposals for me. I got to pick one. If I say no to them and if they ask the reason, what will I say. What will be their reaction if they know that l am a gay? What will mama's reaction.

'You still have seven days, wait till returning from Delhi mama will forget', J&J said

'Every time I am doing this, whenever she brings a proposal since last year. Now it feels like I can't escape from here', Sam said,

Then speak the truth to mama, finish this drama for every day.

It's not that easy, look every mother has a dream to see her son to get married, have kids, play with their kids, live a complete life and I am that unlucky son who can't fulfill her dreams.

Gugu, please tell me what should I do?

I don't know why you human's life is so complicated. Sometimes I feel like we have better life than yours.

We just eat, sleep and dead or killed by humans. I think you should wait for some more time.

Wait! has he fallen asleep? - J&J said

'How can he sleep, if he had to sleep then why he called us', J&J said

Shhh... let's go, let him sleep. In humans it is very rare to sleep peacefully,

'Good night, buddy', Pony said)

Where is Ravi? I am ordering same samosa and tea, anything for you?

'How is Mama?', Lakshya asked

No Improvement, next week we are going to Delhi.

(Ravi arrived)

'Everyday Same Samosa and chai, are not you guys get bored?', Ravi asked.

'These two are best combination ask anyone in India', Sam said

'I think the whole India can be described in thee word its Dosa, Badapav and Samosa, no matter which part of India you go, you definitely can find any one from these three', Lakshya said.

'Forget this I can take you to turkey, right now', Ravi said

Look what I have today, Ta da…

'What is this', Lakshya asked

It's called Baklava, famous Turkish desert.

'Wow looking delicious', Sam said

I made this.

'Ew, I can't see this ugly thing', Sam said

(Lakshya and Sam laughed)

'You know how it made?', Ravi asked

'No, we don't want to know', Sam said

Ignore him...

For that you need special pastry sheets it's called filo pastry sheets or you can make dough and have to cut it thin sheets or you can use Samosa sheets also. Filo sheets are not easily available in market.

Wait, then how you get these sheets.

'Dude, l am working in a five-star hotel. How I cannot find these', Ravi said

I am a chef now, technically not a chef, but for you two l am a chef.

Now bring Pistachio and walnuts roast and grind them. Bring the pastry sheets place walnuts in layer on its top repeat the same process in every layer. Now microwave it. We need a sugar syrup for that also. It's simple, heat sugar, add some water for flavor you can add cinnamon, saffron or Lemon zest. Bring sheets from microwave and add this syrup on the top your baklava is ready to eat.

Did you notice one thing Sam, whenever he talks about a recipe his eyes start to glow. it's like he is not telling the recipe but the recipe represents itself through his mouth.

'And the water from his mouth also telling the same thing', - Sam said

 (everybody laughed)

'You guys Remember Kamala Di in hospital, she was asking about you two', Sam said

If she needs a cook, I am available.

No, for marriage,

She has an elder sister who has a daughter. They are looking for a suitable groom for her. She is beautiful, very good in studying now working in a bank. She was asking if anyone could agree.

Yes, I am.

'But I have one condition. I need Indian in breakfast Italian in lunch and Chinese cuisine in dinner. If she could cook for me that, then I can marry her now', Ravi Said

Shut up.

And what you said - Lakshya asked

Obviously, I said no.

Good,

Guys listen, again, Mama is too serious about my marriage I don't know what to do, everyday same question, when you are going to meet her. Her address and contact details still in my pocket, every evening when I go home, she has only one question with a hope did you meet her and every time I have to tell her a new lie. l am done with this. you guys tell me what should I do.

Then do it, what's problem with that

(Ravi said with avoiding eye contact)

Or say No to Mama, like every time you do.

Now, this option also closed, I have to make a decision. I can't tell more lies to her anymore.

'Then tell everything about you to Mama', Lakhya said

No, can't do that, you guys know that very well.

Look at me, for how long you will fight with you. Just drop your sword and surrender. That is where you will win. If not that, even if you win the world by losing yourself you will get nothing. This battle is not going on somewhere outside that, someone will come to help you. This is completely in your mind; to protect yourself you have created an invisible wall of fear. You have to break the wall of fear then only you can win the war. Once you break the wall you are a winner, then it will doesn't matter if you win or lose against world. you will still be a winner.

What will people say that's different thing, people have always something to say, you have to accept yourself first. I agree society needs to change their thoughts. They will make it worse if they know about you and you can't change that but there is no meaning of life, if you living it by dying every day, you have to live a life as you want to live not as they want you to live.

Fear is good for us. It saves us from doing many stupid things that we always want to do, like fear of accident alert us from whenever we cross our speed limits. It is only good when fear come to save us. But when you take help of fear to protect ourself that moment we get trapped by fear.

You understand what I am saying,

'Yes', Sam said nervously,

When you are going to meet her? - Ravi asked

After the next week maybe, this is address of a yoga center. I don't know much about this, all thanks to Gupta ji. She is learning yoga or something I don't know and I genuinely don't have time to check details about her on social media. I don't have any photo of her, only this contact number.

Ok I have to go now. Mama must be waiting, see you guys.

(Next week in Delhi hospital)

'Mr. Samarendra Barhad please sit', Dr. Nath said.

Thank you doctor.

The way your NGO is doing so much for these innocent souls, it's really amazing and inspiring. How beautiful it could be, when every businessman will do something for nature like you doing.

'You are doing a fantastic work young man; please keep it up', Dr. Nath said

Sure doctor, but we don't have to be a businessman to do something for nature, every single individual should contribute for a better world.

Absolutely right - Dr. said

'Tell me doctor. Is everything ok?', Sam asked.

Mr. Barhad have you ever noticed one thing, whenever an animal gives birth to their child in forest, that new born child depends on her mother for a very short time after it born. In few hours or in few days it stat doing all the things on its own like walk, eat, drink all those things. It doesn't matter if it is a fawn, a baby tiger or elephant. They have to be independent from starting, if the fawn doesn't learn how to run then it will get eaten by any predator same as if the lion cub doesn't learn how to hunt then he has to stay in hunger. Nature has is its law and every animal have to obey it. If not, then nature will not spare them.

You know only we humans are depends for so long to our mother. Is this a revolution process or god's creation who knows? Because we are in hospital then I will avoid the second term - Dr. said with smile, to eat, see things, to understand things right and wrong for all those things we have to depend on someone for so long years that is equal to a complete life cycle for animal, to be a complete human with full grown body and well-developed mind it takes sixteen long years in an average.

For the dependence of so long years, it brings attachments in us and because of the attachment whenever something goes away from us, we feel sad. You know we humans always try to hold things even if we know we can't hold it.

Mr. Barhad what do you think, do plants have same attachment and emotions like human and animals.

I am not getting it doctor, is everything ok?

How is Mama, what is the report says? and to answer your question, emotion and attachments are useless if you can't feel. I am not a biologist or neurological expert, but to feel things you need sensation and above all you need a brain. Since plant don't have brain, I think they can't feel things as we are doing.

Recently a tree was found somewhere in Africa or in Amazon Forest in Brazil I don't know exact location. If you cut any branch of that tree, in few days it will die. According to locals every part of that tree is so connected to each other that, if you cut any part of the tree, it couldn't take the pain of separation. In few days it will die on its own. The reason may something else but the thing is, isn't the same thing happening with humans.

The wound in her leg is not that big, but there is something in her body which holds it from recover. It's like the body don't care anymore about the wound, here I am talking about the same attachment and feeling. It seems like your mother is only breathing. She has no Intension to live. For that reason, the body is also reacting like that. It's a common problem in humans after certain age where they don't find any purpose to live or some past experience repeatedly reminding them their life is not worth for living,

I don't know what happened to her in past, I don't want to know, neither it's my job, but I have seen such many cases where wound is physical but it effects the soul. Now how are you going to handle this, it's up to you. Everyone has different solution for that.

These are some medicines but I don't think, its solution is in this medicine. take care of her.

'Thank you doctor', Sam said

How polluted this city is and the weather is so cold in Delhi, why we have to wait so long in Airports, I am not going to take flight next time and their food, why Delhi peoples are so crazy about momos,

For how long you will act like this, by keeping those things in your heart. It's been more than one and half decade Mama. Please forget those things. Those memory inside your brain, taking everything from you, we are supposed to be happy that those days are gone, why are you still holding those things.

'Are you even listening to me', Sam said

'You don't teach me what to do and what not', Mama said ignoring his words.

You take rest, 1 will cook you something.

Mama I am asking you something, why are you ignoring me?

(Mama went to kitchen without listening him)...

'Again, this electrical issue', Amit said

Our production getting effected by this and generators are taking extra load for that, I have complained many times in their head office. Till now not a single action taken by them. I think we should talk to DM directly. Every time after our complaint they come, fix something but after two three weeks again same problem.

'I already talked with him', Sam said

They have to change the entire phase; it will take some time. They are trying their best to finish this thing with in the time, anyway Amit you should go home now, it's already seven in the evening.

No sir, I can wait till they fix it. Amit said.

Don't call me sir. Just call me Sam ok,

'How is Mama doing?', Amit asked

She is good now; every mother knows everything except, how to take care of themselves.

'Then you should go now', Amit said

No no, it's ok, it's going to end soon.

'So, let's wait in office room than, I am telling Raghu for the tea', Amit said

Sure, Sam agreed

(Ahm... Gugu cleaned her throat and said "someone is jumping inside".

'After very long time he looks so happy', Pooh said

'Why the color of his face changing, oh no someone is blushing', Pony Said

Keep quite you guys, J&J said,

Why the hell you lifting him in air for no reason, let him finish the work and go home Mama is waiting.)

Sam we should think about a different strategy about western region of Odisha. Since our sell is not up to the mark in there. Our two stores are not performing well, maybe we can adopt some old methods to tackle the issue, Amit said

'Not now Amit, it is beyond our work hour, let's Just enjoy the tea for now', Sam said

"The Happie Tails" such a beautiful name

Yes, the kids are working insanely day and night to make this possible. All credit goes to them.

I have heard that guests are coming to "Mahodadhi"- Amit asked

'Yes, three days back we rescued two pregnant dogs, one of them we found in Gutter in a very critical health condition, Luckly we have succussed to save their life. They both are doing well now and soon there will be five or six new guests', Sam replied

Sam, may I ask you a question?

I have been to your home, Three, four times, I have never met your father, is he ok? or he is staying somewhere else.

'You don't have to answer it. If you are not comfortable', Amit Said

(*'Again, that same question. There is something terribly wrong with Humans, you are not going to answer that right?', Gugu said*)

Sam lowered his head and smiled then said,

Do you know one thing Amit, from starting of human life to right this time in every civilization in every period and every stage of history woman are treated as week and inferior. Where men are always treated as strong and superior. I don't know if is true but when God created the world then why he created a man first, why not a woman?

(*'Here we go, the love mode is on. Now you are floating in emotion, you can't answer, there is only tear and pain in that, nothing else', Gugu said*)

You can pick any page of history book; you will find women are always lower than men, ever questioned why?

'Now lam talking like Lakshya, He can talk for hours in this type of topics', Sam said and laughed.

Aristotle in 300 B.C already said that, Men are superior and women are inferior. One governs and other governed and there are many examples like that. Sometimes I wonder from where all these things started? Is this started during the process when we are evolving into Humans or all This started when our brain starts to evolve and we start thinking. I mean when we were apes long time ago, was there also men women mentally in our mind? like male apes should lead the group, take every decision for the group. Back then it must be a power centric world not man centric. I think all these things started after or during our cognitive revolution.

Who started all this, that women will leave her home after marriage. She will take care of her in-laws and everything. I mean it could be reverse like Man could have taken care of home and women could lead the society.

I agree from starting Man has some biological advantages like powerful Muscular body, better analytical thinking and some changes in brain which makes difference from women. From starting of evolution, then after every civilization, only Men are used to go out for food, for war and protect women and child, Men are more capable to handle emotions. Men were used to get education and education was like dream for women.

'Although in every old religion and every civilization you can find female gods. But sadly, they were only limited in Religions believe and Holy books. There is nothing to do with reality. Interestingly for there also only male god is leading, like if you see this in power and compare them, goddess of Rain, goddess of beauty they were all female god. But god of creation and destroy are all superior things are being handled by male gods. Even if today same believe system we can easily find in some religions. If we found such difference among gods then you can imagine the level of discrimination who worship them, Sam said

I agree but you can't compare any civilization to present situation, women are leading in every field now. Biological development or decision making, from leading a country to handling world economy they are handling everything very well not only that they are leading war but also going space too. Although the journey from that stage to this was never easy; to reach here in this stage, all credit goes to them only. In fact, in some fields women are way in front of man, Amit said

Back then women were not getting the stage as today and there was no comparison but it's not like they were completely invisible in that time. You can pick history, was there not battles only for women? When men used to go for a war then who supposed to protect their child, its women. That time also women referred as symbol of success and beauty.

No doubt to get in this stage, where they truly deserving, there is lot of struggles, revolution behind it. Every freedom comes at a cost and sometimes it feels like men are paying for it. Pseudo feminism and women victim card these terms are making news now. We created an invisible barrier. we are so ahead and focused in women development that there is a man non-existing effect created silently.

See it works like this, if a woman runs or Cart at which the sells tea and cookies and we represent her a strong independent woman. If the same thing done by a man, then he is unsuccessful and a failure. Society will Judge them as freedom of choice for her and illiterate for him. They both are doing same thing for same purpose.

Man earns for his family but most of the time women do it for herself only. I am not saying every woman is same, some are also feeding their family too. We can easily find such examples where, how a simple lie of a women can destroy entire life of a man. Maximum govt laws and policies are in favor of women. Is there no domestic violence on Man l am asking you? It is there but it will not come out easily because of the fear of society. Men are tagged himself as strong, they can't express their feeling, his pain. If I am not wrong sometimes women are taking advantages of these things.

In the society where we are living if a man is introvert, then we consider him as dumb. The expectation of being a man is so high that sometimes they weighed down on their own expectation. There was a time where men used snatch Justice and rights for himself but now Men have to beg for their Justice, still they are not getting it. I don't have a problem that everything in favor with women. They truly deserve that. My concern is if you are doing something good for one, it must not be curse for others. -Amit said

Throughout this Journey, how we see things and its perception changed. If a man and women commit, the same crime our first thought for man is, he is guilty but for women it will be, she can't do it. There must be some force of circumstances or necessity. Everybody will try to figure out why she did that. But this 'why' is missing in case of man.

'Oh, it seems like someone to say a lot on this', Sam said

No, it's not like that - Amit replied with smile.

'What I was trying to say is what is been happening for ages, my mother couldn't escape from that', Sam said

I don't understand what are you saying - Amit asked with confusion.

It was a normal, traditional and well-arranged marriage between my father and mother, my grandparents or Mama's parents, I never get a chance to meet them. They already gone before I was born. My Mama was only child and that time being born as a girl was not less than a curse, where girl abortion rate was so high and you can imagine the condition of their education. That was enough when a girl could write her name. In those conditions my Mama completed her primary schooling and all credit goes to my grandparents. Where not a single girl from our village prepared to go school, there my grandfather used to drop her at school in cycle. He was very supportive and progressive. But suddenly my grandmother died and my grandfather began to fall sick and to take care of him, mama took a decision that she will not continue her education. That time she had choice to continue her education in town. As she said, she was only girl from our village who completes primary education and our village Sarpanch was ready to bear all the expense, all the finical expanses and accommodation was taken care by government education scheme. But that time my mother chose my grandfather over education.

I don't know why she did that or whatever she did was right or wrong. lam not even close to Judge her decision. I can't even Imagine the amount of pain she had gone through. Then she got Married to that animal or my father, I don't know much about my father's family neither mama said about them nor I asked once the same.

I only know about the thing was after marring they shifted to another house on rent, my father had an issue with his family for the obvious reason 'money'. Some months after marriage my grandfather also died, now my mama was complete alone.

After around one and half year I born, till then everything was fine but after some years things began to fall apart. Then that demon starts to grab my father's mind. In the male domination world, how can and for how long he can keep himself Isolated. He started yelling and beat my mother in every small thing. He used to spend most of the time drunk at home with every single day It was getting worse. Mama was silent in fear because if she says anything, that creature might hit me as well and I was too small to oppose him. every day I used to pray to God that please end this soon. But there was no one to help me. I was full of questions, why us? We have not done anything wrong to anyone, why God punishing us? My mama used to remain silent.

Right now, it is very easy to say, why she didn't complain against him, why she didn't file a divorce but she had no one in this world except me, I was barely two-year-old. All these feminism things are very effective in this time but it was beyond Imagination on those days. Specially in villages. That time society and their mindset was different, domestic violence was very common on those days. Basically, in India, Husband is always like God to wife. Whatever he does to her she must take it silently. She can't oppose him, if she does, she will go to hell that was the religious believe and society mindset. She can't talk to him in loudly, she cannot oppose him. She can't complain against him.

With time the torture Intensified. He used to drink alcohol whole day and stay at home, no work nothing. He didn't care about us. He used to borrow money to drink, every single day people used to knock our door to get their money back. We can't expect money from my father and Mama couldn't let me die in hanger, for that reason she started working in other's houses. Sometimes in road construction work as daily labor and sometimes in others field. She used to work whole day but before she left, she had to cook for us. So that she can carry some food with her but my mid-day meal was taken care by school. Every evening, she was coming home exhausted and she had to cook dinner for us, most of the time he used snatch her hard earn money by force to get stoned. somehow, she saved something for my admission in school.

One day I asked mama for twenty rupees. So that I can deposit that fee for an exam. If I had passed the test then all my expenses would have taken care by government for from class five to class tenth. My mama said yes, with a big smile. I was very happy that day, when I came back from school that afternoon what I saw, I pray to God no son would see that in his life.

That monster was hitting Mama's face on the almirah. Her face was complete covered with blood and it was also dropping from her nose and a deep cut on her forehead. I ran to save her. Then he threw mama on the ground and start beating me with a rod. He was so drunk that, he had no control what he was doing the reason was obvious. Mama didn't give money him to drink that morning. That day He was someone else. Somehow, he just wanted to kill my mother. That moment money wasn't Important for him but that thing, how dare she said no to him, till the moment a lot of blood had been flown from her body that she was unable to move her body. Then He look around to find something to kill her, but couldn't found anything. Then he tried to push the almirah on her. That seven feet wooden almirah was enough to kill someone if it falls on someone from that height. I gathered all my strength and managed to drag her back but failed to complete drag her and that almirah fell on her leg and it is the same wound that Dr. Nath was saying in Delhi. There was huge sound after it fell down and for that maybe his sense came, he looked around in a strange way. Then he may have realized whatever he was doing wrong. Then he ran away.

Without wasting any more time, I rushed to Lakshy's home for help and Lakshy's grandfather took us to hospital. Till that time, she was not in sense and a lot of blood already flown from her body. I don't know why I Just saw her left hand, she was holding something very tight, when I tried to touch it, she made it tighter so that no one could take it, whatever was in her hand, after sometime when she opened her eyes and saw me in front of her, she loses her finger. It was the same twenty rupees in blood which I was asked for my test this morning. At that moment I cried a lot.

it wouldn't have happened all this, If I wouldn't have asked for twenty rupees.

All the bills paid by Lakshy's grandfather then complaint against him in police station. One or two day he spent in jail after came back from jail he packed his bag and disappeared. He never came back after that neither we tried to find out him, after few months we got to know that he was staying with his parents in his village.

After that incident I promised myself. I would never see tears in her eyes. I will give her all the happiness what see deserves, later realized I am not capable to give her that what every mother wants to see in her life.

('Wait what is He doing? Is he going to tell everything to him', J&J said

He is going to lose Amit also, please somebody stop him.

'No, after long years he found someone to talk about the pain he was holding in his heart, let him speak', Gugu said.)

Suddenly Amit grabbed Sams hand,

('What he is doing', Pony said)

Sam's heartbeat now working like a generator.

You have already gone through a lot. But from now you are not alone whatever happens next, we will face it together.

(Together? what he is saying? - J&J said,

will you please shut up, just listen to him -Pony said)

I never told you that but I also like to spend time with you. We will grow this business together.

(Wait wait, did he just proposed him? what he is doing, is he going to kiss Sam now? -Oh my God, look at his face he is going to kiss him)

Suddenly power restored Sam looked straight into Amit's eyes. These few seconds of eye contact made him to fall again. A fountain of Joyfulness and love suddenly exploded in his heart and the same butterflies in stomach.

'I should go now, it's already late', Amit said and gathered all his stuffs, the nervousness can anyone see by looking his hands.

'That's my water bottle', Sam said

Oh, Sorry,

See you tomorrow.

(Did you see that guys what just happened,

How did he find out about me, may be from Ravi or Lakshya but it doesn't matter, it seems like everything will be fine soon.

'Don't need to Jump out of Joy, maybe it's not exactly what are you thinking', J&J Said

'What's the wrong with you J&J, why can't you see his happiness, we are only his Imagination. He is living This moment so let him', Pony said

'Just look at him guys how happy he is, after so long years we are seeing this happiness in his face', Gugu said.)

'You look different today and you are late is everything ok?', Mama asked.

Call Gupta ji and tell him I am going to meet her tomorrow if she is available.

Are you sure?

You are not fooling me again, right?

No, Mama not this time.

('What are you going to tell her', Pony asked.

'I don't know but I think I am going to tell her everything about me then I am going to tell everything to mama then it will all fine', Sam said.

'This is not going to be easy. Look we are not against anything. We are just saying we can't live life complete emotionally we have to find a balance', J &J said.)

Hello,

'I want to meet Ms. Kamini Dwarika', Sam asked

'She is in Zumba class now, please wait', Receptionist said.

The environment was quite peaceful and energetic at the same time. gym, yoga, meditation, Zumba and Karate classes all are going in different phases.

I was in waiting room corner seat and from there one can easily see the Zamba class because the window glasses were bit open. The class was going on with full passion in typical Bollywood masala music. The teacher was so passionate about what she was doing and one can see her dedication in her face. she was beautiful with usual Zumba outfits, sleeveless top, fair skin and round big eyes not less than any actress from film Industry, medium Ponytail hair and that smile on her face was making her different from other girls. Kamini must be somewhere in this group, any way it is going to end soon.

Hey Sam, a sweet voice interrupted me when I was with my phone.

(Oh, no she is the same Zumba teacher, another self-independent feminist my inner voice told me.)

Just give me five minus then we are ready to go, Kamini said

'Okay, let me bring the car', Sam said.

'No, we don't need that, we can just walk If you one comfortable', Kamini said.

We are going to Starbucks, right?

'Nah, that place is overrated you know how expensive their coffers are, we can drink fresh coconut water, it is in walking distance and you are going to pay for both because you came here to see me ', Kamini said and laughed.

(She is definitely not among other girls, she is really different, she is sweet, no hesitation, very good sense of humor. She is a complete girl and proving me wrong what I was thought.)

Hello? what are you thinking,

Nothing, so it's Kamini, right?

Wrong? Just call me K, everyone knows me here as K.

I thought you are a student here but you are coming out as teacher and trust me you are very good at it.

Thank you,

How are your parents, are they good?

Yes, everyone is fine. My father is in real estate business, and my mother has only job to arrange a well deserving boy for my marriage.

Same here, my mama also everyday crying over my marriage and don't ask about my father.

Why? what happened.

Actually, my father used to beat my mother when he was drunk, one day he decided to kill her but he was out of stock so he went for the same but never came back, it was years ago.

'Don't worry he is never going to Come back', K said with a sad voice.

So, what do you do?

Have you heard the name "Happie tails" I am the part of that NGO.

That means you have no money - K' replied.

 I never said that,

I have a small business also

'What business', K asked.

'Let me give you a hint, everyone's day starts with this', Sam said

Toilet paper?

No,

Brush, paste, perfume, yoga mat.

NO,

'Oh, come on we are not in KBC Set, no one going to pay you for that, just say it', K said.

I run an incense stick company called "Swaroopa"

Are you?

Yes,

No, you are not. Are you really Mr. Samarendra Barhad?

Hello,

Who stand Million Doller company from scratch.

Yes, I guess that me.

Then why are you here, you can easily marry a Bollywood heroine or daughter of a businessmen.

'Because my mama wants to keep it simple. life is already tough; we don't want to make it more complicated', Sam said and laughed.

I have two friends; both are very close to me and I have four imaginary friends. I call them, Pooh the white polar bear, J&J twin squirrel, Pony sweet rabbit, and Gugu a dog.

'Imaginary friend that means they are only exit in your mind', K asked

Absolutely,

That means you are a psycho also.

I don't mind if you call me that, Sam replied.

Why don't you shift your friends from your mind to "The Happie Tails"

No, they are happy there, more important thing is they are away from humans.

('Are you not going to mention about Amit', Gugu asked)

Well, I don't have any that kind of friends. I mean I have friends but not the closest one. The reason is that I love to spend time with myself more.

So, you love to be alone - Sam asked,

'Not exactly, being alone and spend time with myself are two different things', K said

I love doing things like eat in a restaurant, shopping and travel alone. Look lam not anti-social. If any of my friend call me then, I would definitely go with them. I just love more to be with myself.

May I know, why is this? -Sam asked.

I think people live more in social media then real life, I don't have problem with that, they are Just trapped in this showoff culture. That is what I feel. look if lam hungry and lam going to a restaurant or hotel then why I need to click ten photos in five different angles adding four filters. Why I can't Just sit and eat like normal person. Same if I have to buy something, I have budget and whatever I want to buy already in my mind then why would I look for another five shop and if my day was bad, then why I have to put it in my stories, for the attention?

I feel all this very weird, how people could this so easily, as I said I don't have any problem with anything or anyone, everyone has their live. They should live as they want. But this is not for me.

'Seriously are you even girl, you are quite opposite from everyone', Sam said

'Now, I am coming to the point for the reason I agreed to meet with you, I could have said no, and could have given any excuses, but I thought it would be better to talk in person. Despite all, my mother and Gupta ji praised you so much that. If I would say no, then it could have hurt them', K said

I can't do this, in six months there is national ballet dance competition in Chandigarh, contestants from all over India will come. I don't want any compromise in practice, I don't have much time and every box should be checked before time. If I win this competition, Then I will get a chance to represent India internationally, it's my dream. I can't distract myself for this marriage thing.

'Congratulation and all the best', Sam said

I also don't want to get married either. I have some other problem. I don't understand one thing why people are getting married. We are already shortage of food, global warming and many more issues still they are ready to produce next generation.

You don't want to get married and even if I want, I can't marry you

'Why what is your Matter', K asked.

(Is he going to say everything about him to a stranger- Gugu asked)

I don't have any Interest in girls, In case of love and marriage.

What? one of the well-known businessmen and philanthropist in our state is a gay!

(Her expression was funny and shocking at the same time).

You should thank me that lam not from any media, it could have today's headline. She said while trying to hold her laughter.

Whole society making fun of me why would you leave behind. Finish your laugh, lam waiting.

Hey, don't be sad there is nothing wrong with that. it's ok.

So, you are not judging me.

'What are you saying, absolutely not', K said.

I can feel you, with this, live in society. Such a curse. But it's ok one day you will also find someone.

I am sorry but l am getting late for my next class.

She hugged him, and said I think we could be best friends. Person like you is very rare in real life. Please pay the bills, I have some reputation here. Bye. She said with a smile.

'Congratulations all, our all-legal documentation are completed, all the procedure are completed from Animal welfare Board. "The Happie Tails" now has it's our own Identity', Ridhi said

Yes, but remember this is only beginning our MOTTO is "No Hunger, No pain". We have to start next process soon. We have to fast that process of buying vehicle and medical instruments, government also will fund something but we can't depend on that. One thing definitely going to happen is people's trust on us, it will boost our donation.

We have to fast forward the process of giving basic medical training to our volunteers, last Friday we got five calls among them two were critical, we only managed to attend four, we had to miss the last call because it was too far. We have to give training and awareness to locals, whoever wants to help. - Lalit said

It will take two three days more to complete the application. From donation to reward, helpline, success stories, we have to bring all this in one Interface and also, we have to make it user friendly and attractive. So, it is taking more time. In social media we are performing really well, we are getting followers. Everyday peoples connecting with us, we are trying to approach a celebrity or a sports person special from cricket who can campaign for us.

Thank you so much guys all this is possible only for your selfless hard work you guys are handling all this really well. But as Reema said we have put more effort to help them. They need us. We have to spread our work next state also. I know it is not going to be easy but the amount of love and blessing we are getting after treatment and rescue, no money can buy this, this is enough for us.

So, where are we going today?

'Wait, till Lakshy come', Ravi said

Last time Middle East was very sweet.

How is your training going on there! Is everything or? How are your cook partners doing?

'It's chef', Ravi Said

I am still learning to fit in there and absorbing that pressure. Though I am enjoying it completely, look being a chef is not an easy Job. Food is basic need for everyone. There is always a war, in between what our body need and what we really want to eat. A healthy food and the taste, but we all want a tasty and healthy food together. That is what makes tough for a chef. He has to make something which touch the soul. Because a bad food alternatively represents a bad mood. He has that responsibly to cook the dish whose taste replicates the dish itself.

We do work in shifts because there is breakfast buffet, lunch and dinner. We serve the finest art on the table but no one know the battle behind the kitchen door. The amount of hard work we are putting to maintain the bar high, after all that even single thing goes wrong it's on the chef. So, he has to bring that much carefulness and alertness and it comes only with time.

'I think there is very serious discussion going on', Lakshya said.

'Nothing, I was Just teaching him quantum physics', Ravi replies.

Dude, you failed in law take care about your black coat then talk about black hole', Sam said

(Both laughed)

'I didn't fail, I Just dis -Continued it', Ravi replied.

What you have today?

"Bienvenido's a Mexico" (welcome to Mexico)

'It's tacos all the way from Mexico', Ravi said.

We can't have it before you are done so, better hurry up.

It's a Mexican dish, Invented there later spread around the world. Mexico migrants were coming to work with tacos as it was highly portable and cheap. To make it, bring plain flour add olive oil, salt, water make a dough and rest it for some time.

For the Filling we will make "Pico de Gallo" or 'Salsa Fresca' or 'Salsa Crada.'

'We are not in mars, you can say it in our language', Sam said.

It's a Mexican Salsa or in simple we call it salad, it is loaded with fresh tomato, onion, Jalapeno, cilantro and lime juice. Bring a bawl chop them equally squeeze lemon juice then mix it. "Pico code Gallo" is reedy its name is only scary, recipe is simple.

Now bring the dough make it flat by a roller and cut it into round shapes. Heat them in a pan so that they can get its hardness, fold them with that roller In between so that it can have a space for filling. Same as the tissue holding stand that, we usually see in normal hotels. Now air fry it, till complete done. Now bring them, add fillings and enjoy.

'It's just tortilla with Salad in it, there is no special about it', Lakshya Said

Yes. But you can customize your filling, you can add meat, Fish or Cheese as you like.

How is Mama?

She is doing well, two days back she had breathing Issue, doctor said she is fine and with age it comes. I have to take care of her more.

'I met with K', Sam said

'Kamini', you remember that girl, mama forced me to meet,

'Who? That yoga girl?', Ravi said

Actually, she is a Zumba teacher, beautiful, very good sense of humor. She is different from normal girls; I think she is only one in her type. She is educated, well-behaved, talented dancer and more Important is she is full of life.

'This time what was your new lie', Ravi asked.

Not this time, after I meet her, I felt like there is no need to hide anything, so I told her everything about me.

What was her reaction? Nothing, that was the best thing. First time in life I told everything of myself to a stranger and she accepted me as I am. For the first time it felt like, people are not that bad as I was thinking. I am feeling little lite today. We are best friends now - Sam said

So, what's next,

Amit.

Amit? What he did?

Nothing.

Some days before we were talking and I don't know why I felt like he is in love with me.

What? (Ravi reacted with eyes open wide)

Yes,

He said whatever will happen, we will handle it together.

Yes, but how you know that he is in love with you, it's just the normal thing anyone could say.

True.

I saw his eyes, it's not just words someone said, it was more than that and his voice, I felt like someone going to surrender himself completely to me. I was there right in that moment: I can say that he was not lying.

Then what is the problem? You also wanted this right? to find someone like Amit, Now Amit is with you.

'Wait, did he clearly said to you that he loves you?', Lakshya asked.

Nah, but you don't have to say everything to make someone understand what you are saying', Sam replied.

Why are we even talking about this, when something good is going to Happen, Ravi said

Sam, go for it don't look back.

I don't know (Sam said with exhaust voice)

I always wanted this and this is all happening but the fear Inside me is stopping me for this.

'For how long you will live with this fear, it's been a decade, it's enough now. Everything going to well soon, don't bring your fear to this', Ravi said.

No, I am not talking about that fear. that is there. Even if I don't bring that thing to in front of me. There is something that stopping me to accept all this thing happening to me. - Sam said

'I don't get it', Lakshya said.

Look Amit and me together in my Imagination is perfect. we are in love, living a life, my Imaginary world is beautiful but the moment I realize all this thing going to happen in real it scares me a bit. I don't know how the days will be with Amit. What if it couldn't match my imaginary world.

I am happy doesn't matter if it is my imagination only, whatever I am, I am accepted myself, I don't want many things from life. Whatever it is, maybe it is not perfect but there is no sadness or unhappiness. I really don't want any change in my life. I have that fear, I don't know if I call it fear or not, but it is with me. What I want is my one decision shouldn't ruin my present. -Sam said

'Seriously! Is there any kind of stand up going on here? Whatever you are saying it don't make any sense. Come back to real world brother for how long you will live on your Imaginary world', Ravi asked.

You are not getting; it is easy for you. You never been in this situation.

Time!

'It's 6.40 pm', Ravi said

'Only time knows what is next. We only hope for the best', Lakshya said

Oh Sorry - Ravi said

Today or tomorrow, you have to make a decision. You have to choose one or other, even if you not choosing anything. There also you choosing something unknowingly. Just take your time and make a decision, future will hunt you or reward you no one knows. All The consequences only depend upon your choice and don't let anyone choose you for that. No one but your inner you know what is best for you trust that. Take responsibility of your life. Lakshya said

'Oh, enough philosophy for today', Ravi said

Let's order something I can't hold it more.

Is everybody is here? Should you start? This is our first quarter meeting of this year and we are doing well in market and all credit goes to you guys, we will discuss in details later, but now we have to sort out the problems first, Lahar ji, with us and some workers also, let's listen them first. As you all know Lahar ji is the supervisor of all the workers here.

'Lahar ji, please you can rise your issues', Sam said,

First of all, would like to thank you...

'Lahar Ji, you don't have to say it every time. You can skip this part', Sam Insisted.

'No, I have to', Lahar Ji said.

The way you treat every worker here, your care for everyone it's all matters. So, I have to say it.

You always, treat us like your family members. The environment you have created among workers. It's something else, we all know over eighty percent of our workers are women. The facilities you have provided them from sanitation to baby feeding room, all are taken care of by you, from their safety to financial Independence also taken care by the company, not only that this company made them so capable that they can feel the real value to freedom. Their confidence also in next level. They can face any problem in real life outside of the company only because of you. Your decision of sending their salaries to their bank account directly making them financial educated and there is much more, I can't say everything with limited time that we you have in this meeting.

We have only a small request. If there is one more water filter could be installed near storage area it would be very helpful. The persons who work in that area have to walk to Raw material area to drink.

'Lahar ji why didn't any of you raised this till now. You spend all summer like this? you should have raised this before.

Anup, make a purchase order and short this out, anything else? - Sam asked

No sir, Nothing from our side,

Before you ask anyone ask Raghu first, why he denying to give more than ten coffees to me', Anup asked.

Is it true Raghu?

Yes, it is,

(Raghu said with confidence)

everybody started to laugh.

Why?

Ten coffee means ten times he will spend in his private smoking zone. Which is very bad.

Anything from anyone? (Anup said, Ignoring Raghu).

'Oh, this is the reason, Raghu, reduce it to six from next time', Amit said

(Anup give a shocking look to Amit)

No, you can't do it, it's like Immunity to me it's like Alfred for batman, it's like Mark 85 suit for Iron-man, by wearing this he snapped and brought half of population, snatching Infinity stone from Thanos.

'You cannot separate Coffee from me. The Coffee and me both are one', Anup said

What a nice actor you are, Sam appreciated

(everybody starts to laugh again)

Anything from others?

From Housekeeping and transport department?

All good?

Ok, if anything, you guys can contact me anytime.

I have an announcement.

We have decided to create an Emergency Fund for we all. So that we can provide at last 2 months Salary in Emergencies. no one knows what will happen tomorrow, even if our production stops or anything happen to our company, at least everyone will get two-month salary.

How it will work, what will be the structure and the procedure all will be notify soon by Amit.

'Anup, begin working on it', Sam said

That's very good Initiative.

(Everyone agreed)

Lahar Ji and team, you can leave now, it's already late. Thank you for your time.

Thank you, sir, for treating us like this.

Raghu, give them snack packets.

(Lehar ji and workers left)

guys. Let's come to the point

Where are we lagging in western region in our state as compared to other parts in our state. We are doing well in West-Bengal and north east too but not here, anything from you Biren,

No, doubt the quality and Fragrance of our Incense sticks always on the top. The only problem is we are still unreachable to the people.

According to our dealers,

Most of the people live in village areas and they complete depend upon the local traditional market you know, once or twice in a week they gather there in a big ground to buy and sell. They don't go any shopping malls, they don't trust any other shop expect their local market, and this online thing is still far way, Last Qatar there was 4.2 percent from our total sell came from this region out of it, over 80 percent from online only in cities, out of those 20 percent, I would say 18 percent from cities offline and only 2 percent from villages. Most of the villagers Use the local handmade Incense sticks which are easily available in the bulk quantity in their local market.

Another Thing is the package, we have a premium package and in their mindset with premium package it must be expensive but we can tackle that too. The sticks they are using quality is very poor and not good for their health for sure. They Just buy it because of bulk quantity in low price.

Next week I am going there to make them understand how those local products effect their health and will apply our old method to boost sell, one stick in one shop for one hour. We will definitely do well there too.

Okay, do all the needful,

Amit, your turn now.

Go ahead,

So last year we closed around 43 cr. which was our total revenue, where 66.2 percent from our offline and 33.8 percent are from online sales out of that our COGS around 13.2 percent EBITDA 12 percent, our net profit margin will be around 73.7 percent. This financial year on first quarter we are aiming around 10 cr. alone. we are going to close around 70cr in this financial year end.

As we all know we are launching a new product this month three fragrances in one stick and twenty sticks in one packet. It will be very premium for the market so as our target customer. Definitely it is going to very expensive for middle and lower middle-class categories. Let's see how market will react this, it will be 249 per 20 sticks which is 12.45 rupees per incense stick. Our manufacturing cost around 87 rupees and our gross profit will be 162 rupees.

Our gross profit margin will be 65.06 percent. However, customer acquisition cost not included here.

Thank you, Amit. - Sam said

As you all know it's completely bootstrap. Till now we are not gone for any funding, it took around ten years to reach here and without your support it wouldn't have possible. We have walked enough it's time to run we have to cover south of India and it's time to go for International as well.

Next month I am planning, to bring investors in to the board as the CEO and Founder of this company I am ready to dilute 5 percent for 12.5 cr. Which will be 250 cr. valuation of our company. This amount will justify our growth rate in last two, three years, we are still very young it's difficult to give more than 5 percent of equity for the very first round.

What do you think Anup? Biren?

I think we should discuss it one more time I mean look at the market of incense sticks. Our valuation could be more, we are not performing only in excel sheets, we have proven every prediction wrong our growth rate is crazy. If they are not funding us, it's their foolishness but for me it would be 15cr for 3.5 percent of equity which will be around 428.55 Cr.

Thank you, Anup, we will discuss it again it already late, let's wrap this meeting here.

(It was late in the evening till the meeting ends.)

'The sky looks ominous, I think it's going to pour', Anup said.

Before it starts, I have to leave for home. If not, she will very furious - Biren said.

'How sweet, look how much your wife cares about you', Anup said.

Every year we celebrate the day when we first meet as "first meet anniversary"

That's great you know these small things will make the relationship stronger.

'It was yesterday and completely out of my mind', Biren said with lowering his head.

Well, all the best then, only God can save you. you should rush for home now. I also have to fly now - Anup said.

(Rain started pouring down harder and it was extremely windy).

'Amit you should wait, let the rain slow down a bit then I will drop you', Sam said.

Raghu, three cup tea please.

But sir, only you two are here, - Raghu said

'Make one cup for yourself too', Sam said

It's good that all the electrical problems resolved before rain season.

Yeah, they took time but delivered better.

How is your kidney?

'Not good as per doctor', Amit said.

The kidney function starts decreasing and its working on below fifty-five percentage as doctor said. He is saying to start dialysis in next two months. Nausea, tiredness and vomiting happening frequently. doctors indicating for kidney transplant I don't know what to do.

(Amit suddenly grabbed Sam's hand and said,)

Thank you for all this, for medical expenses and consulting best doctor.

'You just take care and do as doctor says, we will figure out rest', - Sam said.

(Is he going to tell him about us - Pony asked

I think he is, it is second time of the month he is going to talk about us after that girl K, he accepted Amit as someone special for sure, because only special persons for him are allowed to know about us, Gugu said.

You guys can't see, he is in love with him. Don't know why he is doing this, only pain is waiting for him – J&J said.

'You two, why don't you guys seal your mouth, if you can't say something good; pony said)

Would you like to meet my friend Pooh? Sam asked

I would love to meet him.

Close your eyes- Sam said, while they still holding each other's hand.

Just listen what I am saying,

"Feel the gentle touch of cool breeze on your cheeks". Everywhere there is white all around, it seems like God himself created this place. The shiny sun above our head and there is only snow wherever your eyes go.

Welcome to northern most part of the globe, welcome to the Arctic.

You know what makes it more beautiful? there is no human here. wherever we go, we humans destroy everything.

Let me take you to a special place.

Look there,

The ruler of the arctic, who owns this place.

The Polar Bear.

The big fluffy giant and most beautiful creature of this planet. look at this mother Son duo, isn't it's cute? for the next two and half years, mother is everything for this cute little cub. They are like shadows to each other. Since the cub is only seven-month-old, he has hundreds of questions in his mind.

Mumma, why these snows are so white?

Because God created it like that.

(typical answer which every parent gives to their child, parents are same wherever we go).

'In upcoming days, you have to learn swimming before that you have to remember every detail about our home', Mama bear said

'I remember everything mamma, there is a glacier, back side of our home, which is going to melt down soon because summer is coming. I am not allowed to go there, to that east seals are coming where we can get food again not to go beyond that where is home of arctic foxes', Cub said with his cute little voice.

Good you have to learn how to increase your smelling power. You have to recognize every smell. You have to observe the direction of wind and intensity of smell very closely. Remember fox always hunt in groups you can't face them alone. What should you do it they find you?

I will run towards water.

They are very sharp and they can chase us easily so that we have to run towards water and for that you have to learn summing.

To hunt seals what we need the most?

Patience, Baby bear replied.

In every thirty minutes they have to come on top for breathing and to warm their bodies they have to come to the surface; to hunt them down you need patience in both cases. Sometimes it may take months to grab a seal so patience.

We can survive on our own from arctic fox, Harsh weather or starving but we can't survive from those two leg monsters. this the battle we always loose.

'What are they and which battle you are talking about mama?', baby bear asked.

That two leg monsters who call themselves humans. They live in another world. they don't usually come here because of low temperature but in recent year they are coming more.

Are they going to kill us.

(baby bear asked in his innocent voice)

If God created snow and it's not hurting us, God also created humans then why they trying to kill us. If I was a human. I would have never killed anyone.

I don't know why they are doing this but whenever you see them just run or try to hide somewhere this white fur works as best camouflage.

Remember patience, wait till they gone in between their conversation a 10-centimeter arrow like something with some liquid attached to it, Hit the ground right below on her back leg.

It's a tranquilizer, they are here, run with me, no matter what don't separate from me.

(mamma bear shouted with fear in her eyes)

They both started to run, in few seconds they found three snowmobiles around them, still they run till their breath out.

Don't stop son, stay with me. don't stop.

(Mamma bear pushed him to run).

Another tranquilizer they shoot with bigger dose but this time that hit her back. they were running with their full strength for two minutes. But in few seconds mama bear's speed starts getting slow. Her feet were not in control. She had no control over her body. In next minute she just slept on the ground. It clearly seems that she wants to run but her body wasn't responding and then she slowly closed her eyes.

Get up Mumma, they are getting closer.

(baby bear trying to wake her up, with full of tears in his eyes).

They are going to kill us Mumma please wake up. Till the time, humans reach there and covered them with a big net. So that they can't run even if they try.

The baby bear saw a human for very first time while trying to cut the net with his teeth.

He saw a barely six feet creature who walks in two legs not even half of a quarter of weight as compared to a full-grown polar bear. Their full body covered by coat something like his own skin, not a single part of their body exposed. Maybe they kill us remove our skin and make their own, baby beer thought. But why they want our skin? Isn't God send them with their own skin? Are they taking skin of all the animals?

Why these humans are so cruel?

Aren't they have a mother? a family? How can they separate us? where they are taking us? to their world or somewhere else? Are they really going to kill us?

Bundle of questions rising in his head while there is no one to answer.

Suddenly a big loud scream interrupted his thoughts a full grown angry polar bear attacked one of these men. He put everything out of anger and so forcefully attacked that the nails completely scratched his jacket and there are eight inch four fingers deep cut mark in his back. Blood starts to flow from it.

Dada...

Baby bear shouted in hope while still in the net. Hanging five ft. about the ground. When there is no chance for his mother to wake up. Baby bear continued to scream for his father.

He starts to attract one by one they were six people. It seems my father is winning and we could go home soon. Baby bear thought.

But then one among them bring a rifle when he saw this bear gone mad and going to kill every one of us.

While the baby bear still scrams for his father out of hope.

Suddenly a loud noise come which was very unpleasant for the snow region and the baby bear saw his father on the ground. The bullet hit right on his shoulder and there was complete silence.

The baby bear was completely frozen for a moment. In few minutes his family completely destroyed by these cruel humans. why they are doing this to us. We never saw them before neither we did something wrong to them still why they did it to us.

Now they got time to warp up things, load mother and son bear on a truck and start moving.

But his father, he hasn't done yet. He bring all his strength together and start chasing them. He was almost out of blood and the snow-white surface becomes red; with every step he is losing every drop of life. But not ready to give up.

He had no idea where they are taking to his family. He had no idea whether he is going to find them back or not. One thing he is very clear about that he had to protect them till his last breath.

One of the men slowed the vehicle and said" Look how hard he is trying to save them" and animals do have feelings. Let's end this here"

He brought his rifle and shoot two times, one hit above his nose and other hit right his head.

The big giant innocent soul gone for a sleep forever all alone. That's my friend Pooh.

Now open your eyes and clear your tears.

'The sky is clear now and rain had stopped let me drop you', Sam said

Amit agreed and said ok, with clearing his throat.

How is she? Is there everything fine between you two? How much time will you take? if it was our time, we would have a child by now.

'Everything is fine mama, yes about the child thing I can agree', Sam said and laughed.

Bring home her someday. I also want to meet her.

I will mama but she is busy for her competition. It's only few months left. She is only focusing on that. marriage is not a small thing; everyone has their life; she just needs some time.

(Again, one more lie, for how many times do I have to repeat this. I have no idea)

You just take care of yourself do as the doctor said. Everything will happen on its time. Let's have dinner.

There is an invitation for you from our health minister. He is going to arrange a massive party for his daughter's 16th Birthday.

Of course he will. Half of the city's money controlled by him; in some way he has to spend it. Will you go with me mama?

Have I missed a single of your parties till now?

Mama said sarcastically.

'You can say it directly mama, you don't want to come. Take your medicines and take rest', Sam said

(So, what is next? Gugu asked what are you going to do now?

What am I going to do? Sam repeated

How simple this question is, you put some words together and add a question mark in the end. But if it is so simple then what makes someone so hard to answer it. Maybe it holds future on it or really you just wait for something to happen on its own. But it's not that simple sometime it works but not every time. In life most of the time you have to make a decision, set a plan or make a choice.

What about the answer 'I don't know'. why it feels like a quit good answer for every question.

'It is', Gugu said.

But look at this closely it holds a sense of surrender in it. It holds a fear and a confusion in it. If you say 'I don't know' that means you didn't even try to figure out the answer. Which could be better answer then 'I don't know'.

Why future or fate will decide for you. While you have a solid present in your hand. You only know what is best for you. Take charge of your life take decision which is best for you and bring the courage to face the consequences whether it is good or not and remember one thing you can't control everything.

It's not that easy Gugu -Sam said

To take a decision choose something which is best for you out of many, nothing wrong with that but we are humans emotionally connected with each other. Sometime it is curse for us. But that is a beauty for us too.

If you taking a decision then definitely it will affect others you can't escape from that. Either you take a decision for you by hurting others or make everyone happy by hurting yourself. There is no other way. You can't make everything perfect. Even if you could do it for a moment still you don't have any idea what tomorrow will bring.

But you have to make one -Gugu said.

Yes, I have to -Sam replied.

It was one smooth evening in July and rain already has done his work. The sky is clear now and stars were glittering. It was one of the best cafes beside the riverfront in the city. This cold wind reminds that spring evening when she decided not to look back.

Good people and perfect world only exit in stories there is no fairy tales in real. the world is full of monsters with gentleman's skin. Once they remove the mask you will see their real face.

'Sorry I am late that voice interrupted her thought, it was Sam'.

'No, it's fine I am with my second coffee only', K said angrily.

This slow music and the view will save you today not next time - K said.

Any way you can order whatever you want.

'Is it your angry face? It looks funnier than your real face', Sam said and laughed.

How is your practice going on?

I have to put my hundred and one percent. I have to give my everything to be on top three. That only clear my international ticket.

You must be proud of your toe - Sam said.

(both laughed)

What about you? How is your NGO? "Happie Tails" right?

How is Amit?

He is not well still struggling with the issue in fact doctor already said to search for a donor.

I am sorry, it must be tough for both of you.

Nah, its fine. Once we find the donor everything will back in place.

On the other hand, I think we are doing very good on the field also. Every single day is a new challenge for us. Last couple of months was very tough all thanks to rain, it is not easy in the seasons, specially like remote village location where they don't even have a solid road to get there in time. To be there in time is a challenge itself. After that give treatment to them there, or bring them to shelter for better treatment is not easy.

But all credit goes to the young team. They are doing it selflessly from social media awareness to give training to locals for basic treatment. They are on the top, though there is no competition but still the amount of effort they one putting hats of them. for those efforts we start to recognize internationally also. Very much appreciated by state and central government and other originations also.

Last week we had a call that, a big giant bull was stuck in sludge near a village called Kasumi twenty kilometer from here, they said there is many injuries in his body, he is so exhaust that he is not even trying to escape maybe he was trying since last night or more. that place was bit far from village where nobody usually goes. By the time we reach there it was still drizzling and there was no road for that spot. No vehicle can go there and we had to walk ten minutes. That road was muddy and slippery that all are struggling to walk normally there both side tree and full of long grass that we had to clear it by hand while walking to see the next step. Hates off to Reema who was leading us.

Before us ODRAF team was already there, in Odisha this team is especially active in this four-five month due to cyclones are coming frequently. They were waiting for us. There are multiple injuries in his body and they don't have any medical expertise.

He is been there more than twenty for hours Tusar said, our medical head the wound on his forehead looks normal but that on the right side of his neck need to treat immediately, it was below the road. We have to pull him out as he can barely open his eyes. But it was not easy to pull a big adult bull with this slope, it was clear any one can guess, there was a fight between two bulls. Foot prints were still there, other one must have pushed him and he slide down but when he tried to escape the more kick his legs the deeper, he gone there.

Lucky, the front two legs are clearly visible but problem is that neck is wounded we have to make a plan to avoid more damage. ODRAF team came up with a plan. Two of their man will go down with two ropes. Tight the rope among his body that all pressure will take leg joints and hump, that was not also easy to lift both of its front legs take the rope below the leg and belly in middle of muds, but we had the finest team from disaster management.

Five ODRAF member, four of us, five local villagers. We divided into two each of seven people with number and with muscle power. We can't let Reema, Tusar and Somesh in one team because they are kids in first attempt, we failed again after sometime in second attempt we also failed but in third when he realized someone trying to save him. He put all his strength, not even he came out from mud but also covered the distance of the slope. In the next minutes he was in top solid land. He can barely stand immediately he let down. ODRAF unbound the rope and Tusar started his medical work. It took one and half hours to complete this.

'That is really very inspiring', - K said.

I have a question if you don't mind. Why are you doing this? I mean whatever you are doing is great but you have everything in life name, fame, money. why are you still choosing to do this in every alternate day?

'Because they are not humans', Sam said.

It seems that someone has a big issue with humans.

No, I don't have any problem with humans. It's just that we humans have everything and a problem with everything, animals are simple. They are happy if they are full. You just feed them and they are all yours. They are not playing with each other's emotion. They don't run their brain for economic development by destroying nature. They are not pretending which they are not, like humans.

That's true - K said.

You know what is the best part was when we finish our work, rescue treatment and all and coming back after few steps when I looked back, he was seeing us. those shiny teary eyes says it all. They show their gratitude to us no matter if it is a dog, cow, cat or a bull. Exactly that moment when you realize that you are doing something good. something that completes you, a state of satisfaction, a fountain inside your heart, that moment which stays only few seconds, that pushes me to do more.

Apart from that emotion, if it's not me, not you then who? someone has to stand with them, world is busy in economic crises, countries are busy with Border Issues. Humans are busy with God issues. I am not doing a favor to them neither I am doing something great, I am doing this because I could do this and I will do this.

You know, you should come with us one day.

Definitely, I would love to,

Where are they? supposed to come by seven, it's already seven fifteen.

They will Join shorty. Would you like to order somethings. Coffee is already cold.

I hope you are not getting late, Sam said

Nah, no hurry, only my mom has an issue, she has clear instruction, wherever you go, come before ten. my Mama also same.

Tell me one thing, how do you manage all these things you have a huge valuation company, a well-established NGO. Personal life, How This twenty-four hour works for you?

Simple it works for me because I am selfish.

"Selfish! I don't get it', K Said.

Sam laughed and said,

If you looking to hear something motivational, you know something like to scream and say why you think you have twenty-four hours while you have eighty-six thousand and four hundred seconds, make every second count. Make every second work for you, you could do this, you could do that, if you really want to hear something like that, then I am not the person...

(They both laughed)

Look, when I say l am selfish, I started a company because I was the man who needed money the most, I did it for myself only. I contribute to the Economy or eighty percentage of our employee are women that's different thing, me and my mom knows what not we have done to reach here.

Hunger is the biggest motivator, when your basic becomes your dream, and every next day a new person kicks your door, because your beloved father borrowed money from them, when a two-time meal becomes your aim, a rope which can carry your weight becomes your vision. When your existence becomes a question mark and survival is your basic need, at that moment motivation also give up on you.

You do it or not do it no one cares. Your life doesn't matter to anybody and I decided to do this alone. I don't have any complain to anyone. The problem was mine so I am the one who had to figure out something. At that stage you can't say that I don't have much time or the world is against me, but at that moment you become fearless also, because you have nothing to lose.

So, yes, I did it, I did it myself. So yes, I am a selfish

When barley twenty days old puppy was brutally killed by a drunken man, that puppy had only one mistake, she didn't take permission before entering the gate in search of food. Where humans were performing pooja and these so-called good people from progressive society and polished civilization acted like nothing happened and that Innocent life was nothing to them, I had a problem with that, I decided to do something for them and that became "Happie tails" now.

Again, that was my problem. I couldn't act like these gentlemen, for me every Innocent life matters. I did it for myself so that no Innocent soul lost his life by accident or be killed by human.

So, yes, I did it for myself so, I am selfish.

One good thing Happened is that, we connect people through emotions, they are like if this company doing something good for animals, they are honest so as their product. which is right, to be honest apart from the marketing, advertising this is one of the factors which boosts our sales and this is also true that I spend on "Happie Tails" more than earning, if you consider only this factor but that doesn't matter.

'That's great', K said

I have only last question for you, since they are still not here

Yeah, go ahead.

How you started all these? There are more than fifty videos on YouTube about the case study of your company.

Really?

You don't know that?

'No, I am aware of that but the numbers are surprising', Sam said

I am not trying to be modest but to be honest I don't get much time for this.

I am sure everything they are showing in their videos is not correct. They Just add something on their own with some dramatic background music for the views.

'I want to hear it from you', K insisted

From the man himself, only If you comfortable with this.

I was in fifth standard when my father left us. Somehow, I completed my twelfth and all credit goes to my Mama. She did everything to make sure, complete my schooling, whatever I am today because of her. That time I was seventeen and I can't see someone putting all the effort for my better future, while our present was middle of nowhere. That stage of my life I realized that for a better future you only need two things money and education.

These are two door which can open a great future. One was already closed for myself and the Second door I closed for myself in my hand permanently.

For next two years, I did everything what I could do, road construction to making building as a daily worker, cleaning sludge from houses, working on others field. That time legal age of work wasn't strict and all those things I was doing had only one purpose to close all the debts. So that no one knock our door further. My mother used to work other's houses. For two long years we had no life for ourselves, no festival. no celebration, no happiness nothing. We had only a schedule eat go to work earn money pay debt, sleep and repeat. It took two and half years to clear all the debts, it was relief from me, a freedom. it was like someone give me ticket and spoke. 'Go and Sleep' now you can see your dreams, you can live a life, it's like your exam is over and you don't even care about your result.

'But why you choose to make Incense sticks, there were hundreds of things you could have tried,

'Now it feels like I am in an interview panel.', Sam said and laughed.

'I am sorry but your life story making me more curious', K said

Back that time, I had no option to choose something. I had to do whatever I get but yes, I tried different things. But all I can say that, I didn't choose anything but it chose me.

Look here in India whatever you do you never forget to show your gratitude to God. I am not talking about our generation but it is happening every day in every home. No matter how terrible the night was, never forget to give the thankfulness to God. They offer their gratitude for a better day. They do it for a hope that someone is there who is taking care of them who is Supreme and one day he will make everything all right.

Incense sticks are being used for fragrance which is obvious but it serves different purpose at different places like in home, temples and Churches. A mild incense fragrance has a power to shift your mind into more stable and relax state. According to some scriptures you are going to smell a lot of it in Heaven. In Old Testament there is sacrifice of incense mentioned.

In temples incense sticks are used for worship of God, different number of Sticks are used for different purpose. There is still debate of using bamboo in incense sticks in Hinduism. Burning a bamboo creating a negative impact in environment and after death of someone during his last rights four people carry the body to that place where he has to be burned by temporary bed made from Bamboo and they had to carry it with their shoulder at that place they burn the bodies but not the bamboos. So, some place doesn't burn Bamboo in puja it is a sign of last journey of life.

Incense sticks being used way before from us for different purposes. and there is a demand for it every time. everyone has a faith and a way to show their gratitude. I am Just fulfilling the demand.

Okay understood - K said

'But how did you started what are the challenges you faced? please say it from beginning', K insisted

'I will but I have a request ', Sam said

Make her believe that we are going to marry soon.

'What', K shocked.

No, I can't do that,

This is not right, you can't break her faith, last time we already discussed about it, you have to accept the truth.

I know, Sam said

It is difficult for me too, she has seen everything in her life, now she has everything but still empty Inside. Now she has only one wish "my marriage".

Then what's wrong?

'Marriage will be there only difference is Amit will be there in place of me', K said

You know what's wrong. -Sam shouted.

She has only one wish and for the first time she is asking for something to me. How can I say No?

I understand but you tell me for how long this will go on like this and don't worry I will meet her.

I don't know, Sam said, in hopeless voice I will figure out something later.

What if it will not work?

Just say the truth and settle the thing forever.

So, tell me what should I do to Impress her like a real daughter-in-law.

Nothing. My mama is very sweet and innocent you just meet her as you are only one thing you have to do is,

What?

Don't tell the truth to her,

Ah, don't worry it's you who is going to do that.

'I hope we are not late', Lakshya said

Late? of course not,

You guys can't be late. She is about to finish her third Coffee. you know what, you are not late time must be ahead of you guys.

Are you done?

Don't try to be Sarcastic, it doesn't suit on you. Ravi said

This is 'Kamini' and 'K' this is Lakshya and he is Ravi our future Michelin Star Chef.

'The weather is quite Romantic, no? two love birds here, going to get Married', Ravi said

(Lakshya chuckled)

Ha...ha...Very funny - Sam said

Ravi also laughed and said, you know I have to change it, I have to act serious in serious situations.

'No, you don't have to, you are blessed with that', K said

I was Just curious how he started all this, and for now we are not done yet,

For that you need a tissue paper. There is Lot of pain in it, whenever there is an issue, there is a tissue.

"Issue-tissue" you guys getting it?

No, no, please stop it, it's not even funny, you Just making it for no reason - Lakshya said

tell me what do we have today?

You know 'K', Ravi is a trainee in a restaurant which serves international guests and whenever we meet in weekend he come up with one international dish.

'With making process', Sam interrupted

It's called recipe, Ravi objected

Sorry Mr. Gordon Ramsy, please continue,

Today, I will take you guys to Mount Fiji, get into the bullet train, put your seat belt on.

'Nihon e Yoko so'

Ta...da... welcome to Japan.

It is sushi, right? K asked

Nope it's Japanese Authentic Sushi -Ravi said

So, you guys ready?

Please take notes, not a single point should be missed

Show off -Sam Murmured.

For the recipe we need short grain rice. Rinse for two or three times. Bring a cooker put some rice and same amount of water on it and let it boil after that low the heat for fifteen minutes. Then turn off the heat and keep it like this for ten minutes. You can use a glass lid cover to see its boiling and when to slow down the heat. Usually in home we don't have that but we can see that by removing lid, it's ok if it became bit sticky and messy. You are making Sushi not Biriyani.

Now we have to make some seasoned vinegar, for that we need rice vinegar add some salt and sugar in it according to your taste. You can make it sweeter, more or less salty or sour according to your taste palate. Just mix everything with very low heat, let the sugar and salt completely dissolve, you can make more and store in fridge for further use.

Now bring the boiled rice to a pot and add ten percent of seasoned vinegar compared to amount of rice you are taking. Make sure every single grain of rice gets its coating of seasoned vinegar but do it very gently as it is still hot and let it cool down to room temperature after mixing.

Take a seaweed, it is basically ocean grass or shrubs. They typically grow in shallow water near coastal areas. Cut the seaweed as you like square or rectangular. Now we have to make balls of seasoned vinegar rice which can spread equally on the seaweed sheet, to spread, place the ball of rice middle of the sheet, don't push it to spread, just spread it gently with your fingertips so that it can spread evenly on the sheet including corners. Add some sesame seed then flip, now add the veggies anything you like but cut them in long strips so that it can fit in sheets. You can add anything like cucumber, carrot, yellow paper, avocado, asparagus anything you like.

Now the complicated part comes the rolling part; to roll the prepared Sushi, you can use the index finger and thumb of both hands. Once you did it with one side of the sheet and it's easy to roll it further. Bamboo mats basically used to press and squeeze both sides, the sheet is on the top or the rice, doesn't matter but veggies must be inside the roll. Now cut it into small bite size rolls, dip in soya souse and enjoy.

One green paste that goes on the top of Sushi, is one of the most expansive Ingredient and that is called Wasabi. Most of the restaurants and hotels only tries to duplicate the original taste of Wasabi by adding different ingredient like, horseradish, salt, corn starch, Soybean Oil, Mustard Oil and Sweetener and more with different amount, while wasabi powder is only one percent in it. Real Wasabi is hard to come across and it can cost two hundred and fifty dollars per kilograms. Wasabi is a small green plant in Brassica family it is similar like horseradish but it smaller than it about ten to fifteen centimeter in length and half of its weight, The reason it is so rare is that it is hardest plant to grow commercially in the world. The only place in the world where it can be found growing naturally is alongside Japanese streams, where has the specific condition it needs to thrive. It needs continues supply of water. It can only tolerate the temperature eight to ten degree all year around and takes 18 Months before it can be harvested and everything is done by hand.

To use Wasabi, it has to scratch in a grater and collect the paste. It has to break down to its cellular levels to find its fresh taste.

Most of the people who eats Sushi don't have any Idea the actual taste of Wasabi except the green color paste which is being used all around to replace Wasabi. The actual wasabi tastes like bit more gentle, little bit more like earthy, almost like sweet after taste and way more pleasant, while that green paste tastes like mix of Mustard and Horseradish. If you take a piece of Wasabi and eat like carrot, you won't get the real taste. you have to break it down to Cellular level to find its reactive pure taste.

Now comeback to Sushi there are variety of Sushi in Japan like Nigri, Uramaki, Hakozushi, I Kura and more. Uramaki Sushi also called Inside out Roll, it rolled so the nori sheet is on the inside and rice on the top side. Like this which are on the table. In Hosomaki sushi is thin Sushi rolls cut it into perfect bite size pieces. Those cute little Rolls are filled with only one ingredient usually vegetable or fish to create a lovely pop of color in center.

My favorite sushi is Tera maki Sushi or Hand rolled Sushi. It is most common and very casual way of making Sushi, no special equipment no fancy Stuff just add your favorite veggies as roll it as you like and eat it.

'That's cool you are master on it', K said

'We don't just cook, we represent food as whole', Ravi replied

Are you done? can we just eat now? - Sam said

Every time same drama,

Ignore him. He is just Jealous of me, Ravi said

What about you Lakshya? - K asked

I am pursuing psychology - Lakshy replied.

He has only one mission. Make everyone "Yogi"

He is a philosophy teacher also.

Really? That's Interesting K said surprisingly.

Yes, He is giving free philosophy classes to students from class eight to twelve.

How? as far I know there is no philosophy subject in their syllabus.

Yes, but he added this one himself, don't you know one of the private school networks running by his father.

No, it's not like that, it's completely optional, once in a week for one hour. It is completely depending on them if they want to attend or not. But surprisingly most of the classes are not empty as you guys excepting -Lakshy said

Okay then, you guys please carry on. I got to go. She must be waiting for me', Sam said

Lakshy? are you coming Health minister daughter's Birthday party this Friday?

Yeah, papa is not well, so I have to.

Are you guys talking about Urvi's birthday? K asked,

'Are you coming? I don't know her name to be honest', Sam said

It's Urvi and l am her yoga teacher and I have personal invitation so I have to come.

And the Entire menu designed by our team, Ravi said

You are also coming - K surprised,

Obviously if not then who will cook there.

That's great, we will meet there, bye

(Sam left for home)

"I don't understand why people celebrate Birthdays? Ravi said,

'Do you have a problem that minister is giving a huge party?', K asked

No, I don't have any problem with that, for his reputation and amount of money he has, where most of it not belongs to him, he deserves to give this kind of party.

I am talking about every individual, what is so special about Birthdays, why are they excited from months ago, and their planning, I mean you tell me is that make any sense for what reason it is so? Just because you born on that date? What is your contribution on that? Your parents did something and you just popped up, then why this celebration. - Ravi said.

Okay but why you have any problem with that it's their birthday, they will do whatever they want to do everyone has their own rights.

'I don't think they are creating any problem with that', Lakshya said

Of course they are, can't you guys see that, they are creating an unseen boundary. If you are celebrating your birthday, making plans for it. Throwing cake, each other then you are cool. Look at their social media, it shows they have everything, they are only living a life. While if someone doing his work sincerely, supports his family, have responsibility, he is a looser, according to our society they don't have a life and they are dead inside this is the unseen boundary they are creating by showing such things off.

Agree but look at the other side of the story everyone wishes you, you meet each other after a long time, have conversations, having fun together, everyone is busy in their life but this is the day in a year where you involve completely.

But it could be any other day, why it's Birthday only? I am telling you, do a thing, call your friends who is joining on your birthday every year and tell them, "You are promoted and salary hiked by thirty percent and planning to buy a house next month. This is a success party from my side you guys Just have to come".

I can assure you that halt of your friends will say "I will try" and half of them will come with bunch of questions, you will see party is there, friends also there but the fun is missing. It could have something else, if it was your birthday. They don't care about your personal success, no one cares.

We are humans. We are happy as long as someone not ahead of us.

'K, what do you think about it', Ravi asked

I think I should go now, it's already late, supposed to be there, in home before ten.

Wait Lakshy will drop you,

No, driver already waiting outside.

You got a car and driver too, then there is rich girl poor guy love story not possible because you both one rich here. -Ravi said and laughed

Shut up,

See you there in Party Guys, Good Night.

How was the day? Gugu asked,

Same nothing to celebrate, tired reply came from Sam.

'He is not playing with us anymore. I think he is not loving us anymore', Pooh said

'Yes, he is changed. He got some new friends out there', Pony said.

It's not like that pooh, Okay Pony let's play,

You suggest, what game we should play?

'Hide and Sick', 'Chor Police' anything you like.

'What's wrong with you guys, it's already three in morning let him sleep', J&J said

'Are these two, Okay? What happened to them, how they talking so nicely tonight', Sam said.

(J&J give a look to Sam)

No, it's good, being good and nice to everyone is always good.

(Sam said with avoiding eye contact with J&J)

'You know what, do whatever you want to do play or sleep, just don't Include us', J&J said.

Are you going to tell her about Amit?

I don't know Gugu and I don't want to talk this night now.

But someday you have to face it.

Yes, but not today.

'Namaste aunty', K said

Please come finally you are here, you have no idea how many times I have told Simu to bring you here, you are more beautiful than the photo which I have.

Thank you, Aunty,

It's raining outside and weather is cold, let me make you a ginger tea.

'it's okay Aunty, I am good', K said

Simu, check the internet it's not working since morning.

Simu? K tried to guess,

It's Samarendra Barhad, friends call me Sam but only Mama call me with this name. Simu,

How are your parents?

They are good, My mom keeping herself busy in yoga and Kitchen stuff and papa mostly out of town for the Business thing.

I prepared 'Gajar ka Halwa with desi ghee' for you, I hope you like it. it has less sugar but more love, I don't understand why today's kids are so obsessed with diet and fitness thing.

I don't have an Issue with that Aunty, I eat everything what I like.

Tell me what do you like on lunch?

'Anything Aunty. I am not going anywhere without having lunch with you said', K said

Nice house Simu, the Interior looks quite expensive.

Thank you,

Rain has stopped, Let's go to garden area my mom spends most of the time here. Mom has pretty good knowledge about this farming thing. This section is for herbs and on your left complete vegetable section. We don't usually buy veggies from outside. This garden has everything what normal Indian family wants in their kitchen.

That's why she needs internet for learning and she is very good at organic Indoor farming and fertilizer thing.

Come with me I want to show you something, look at this,

Wow... So many birds,

Nah, don't step further. They will fly away. They only allow my Mama close to them.

Is that Indian sparrow, I am seeing this bird after so many years. Aren't they being in extinct list.

Yes, all credit goes to humans and their concrete forest.

'Look at these white pigeons, Parrots, all looks so colorful here. There is no cage here. How they living here together?', K asked

Because it's not a zoo. They are only here because they feel safe here. Although my mama giving them luxurious facilities. Look at these artificial branches. She colored them like wood so that the birds can feel familiar. The roof saves them from sun and rain, every day she cleans this place, pour fresh water and give them food.

That's so sweet, now I can see how is your love for animal came from.

You can rest now. Let me resolve the internet.

Aunty may I help you with something?

You know cooking?

No, but I can help you with taste dishes. I am an expert in that, you know aunty whenever my mom is cooking and I am in home we talk a lot about everything in kitchen, about our neighbor, about our society aunties, about my work and whenever papa is in home we both tease him with making fun about his work and his side relatives.

'But have you ever tried to hear something that your mom never said?'

Han?

No, nothing. Just pass me the cumin seeds,

Here,

It's fennel.

Oh. Sorry it looks so similar.

Aunty, may I ask you something if you don't mind,

'In these days I don't mind in anything anymore', mama said with a fake smile.

How did you survive from those days? from marriage?

Yes, Simu told me everything.

Why didn't you protest for yourself, why did you accept all that? If you get a chance to change your part, what would you like to change.

(clearly anyone can see a thin layer of tears in her eyes, she smiled said,)

What would I like to change? Actually, it's nothing, it's my past and I don't live there anymore. You are still suffering or survived, it was you who completes you not the situation. I am not saying to stay quiet and let everything happen to you I am just saying the other side of the same thing. Negotiating with time.

But aunty everyone has a choice for every situation, right?

'Choice' is a heavy word for some people, let me tell you a story,

Once there was a king who had everything great ministers' group. Beautiful wife, harmony in his states, great relation with neighbor states peace all around. But somewhere he fed up with these things and decided to travel some new place for someday with his wife, but not as a king but as an ordinary man. So, no one could recognize him and his wife.

Now he had many options for a right place to visit but some places are rejected by his wife, some places are rejected by the king himself and some are by both.

This is the problem with choices the more option you have, the more confuse you will get, in end the king and his wife ended with going nowhere.

Now see, if you are drowning, will you really look for a choice, you just grab anything, no matter it's a rope or a snake. This choice thing making life more complicated.

'But aunty choice is there only to make life easier so that you can choose best for yourself', K said

really?

Have you seen animal inside zoo, employees who take care of them must give them food, now that animal has a choice, whether he will eat or not.

What do you think, what will he choose?

Definitely he will eat, if not then he will die in hunger.

Exactly,

Sometimes when we look others and assume why she took that decision? While there were many better options for her, but only she knows what she has to go through to make that decision. But somehow you have to pick one. Now look this closely when you are picking an option or taking a decision your current situation, fear of future, your past everything involves in it to make a choice.

For the world you may have many choices but you only know the true difference between make a choice or forced to make a choice like that animal in the zoo.

And in my case "I choose, not to choose anything"

But…

No more questions, Lunch if ready let's eat together.

(They had lunch together and K is about to leave)

Thank you, aunty, for the delicious meal.

Here, take this

What is this?

Your favorite 'Gajar ka halwa' and it's not for you, you had enough, take it for mummy papa, and listen, keep these too.

'Wow how beautiful these earrings are and its pure gold', K said

Aunty please I can't take it, this is enough for me I can't handle this much love.

These are of my mother's. since I don't have a daughter, you keep it.

(K started crying and hugged her)

Simu, drop her and remember next you will come to my home only after marriage.

(Mama said with a hope inside)

I am kidding, you can take your time.

'Okay then let's go', Sam said

Wait, don't take your car,

Can we just walk for a while

Sure,

'I can't do this to her, it's not right, I cannot break her trust. She is so sweet. What would be her reaction. When she will know the truth?', K said

'Honestly I don't know', Sam said

She is very happy right now; this is the only thing matters to me now.

Remember your story was incomplete that day, it's time to complete.

Which story?

If you are thinking something miracle, extraordinary happened in my business, it's not like that. I am just fulfilling the demand and get some profit out of it.

'I still want to hear', K said.

After my father left us, I got to do something. Somehow, I completed my twelfth Lakshy's grandfather guided me to do something stable, the problem with being a daily worker was that someday you get work and someday not. Actually, he gave me the idea of making incense sticks. So, I borrowed some money from him and started. I had no intension to scale it up or growth the business at that time. I only just had one goal to sale more incense sticks so that we can arrange the food for next two days.

Started with basic by buying raw material with very small capital. To make the incense sticks we need charcoal, which is the main ingredient then wood dust, josh powder for binding and potassium Nitrite to improve quality and resolute burning issue.

For the making, first we have to prepare the premix powder and for that we mix these things with different quantity with water according to the batch you are preparing. Now these mixtures had to roll over in Bamboo sticks. This is the incense sticks usually makers buy to skip the premix process but it has no fragrance. We have to add that fragrance later and it a different process.

My mother and me used to roll the mixture over the stick by hand. Usually, machines are used to make these because by machine we can get nice uniform coating. It was tough to do with hands, sometimes the mixture was dry or too liquid in both cases it will create problem during rolling. The process was simple, but execution was difficult. You have to take small amount of mixture keep it on the middle of the sticks and roll it on a plain surface gently so that it can spread uniformly on its own, even if we got a perfect mixture, we have to maintain same amount of uniform coating from start to end on the stick. Sometimes its heavy in one side and very thin in other.

I still remember on first day, we together made only nine good sticks in one hour.

Next step is to add fragrance on raw incense sticks, for that perfume and dip oil required, we need a clean barrel so that no other perfume can mix with it. Add perfume with dip oil on that barrel, the ideal ratio is one and four. Now seal the barrel and shake it well so that they can mix properly and rest at least forty-eight hours. Now the process is called dipping ratio which plays important role in making incense sticks. Take one-kilogram incense sticks and dip it on the perfume mix which was in rest for two days. Just dip is completely and gentle shake it for twenty seconds. Make sure every single stick on that bundle get a proper dip, you can check it by taking one stick from middle of the bundle. Rest these sticks for six to eight hours, now weight it again it should be one kg two fifty to three hundred grams, that mean one kg incense sticks which was raw, socked two fifty to three hundred grams of perfume. If it soaking less than that then you will not get the smell, if the soaking more than that, then it will dent on your wallet and it will have more smoke after burning.

Now everything is changed. Most of the work done by machine we have a new process of making incense sticks. use of charcoal reduces to ninety percentage in our making now we use flower instead of those powders we are now well-known brand and it's a different recipe now we are adapting which I can't share.

Throughout the journey from there to here was not easy for us. This ten year was full of challenges. I just keep doing what had to be done, for that process the very first thing what I did was study the perfume, because that is the core thing. If your sticks don't smell good then why would anyone will buy it. Offering to God is a next thing before it must give you that relaxation with its smell. I studied about the notes and accords of different perfume, with one smell you can't please everyone, everyone has different taste of smell. I had to figure out that one smell which can be approved by most of the people. It was very complex process later we added two smells in single incense stick.

Sense of smell is like sense of taste for that we have a special organ of our body, ability to smell comes from specialized sensory cell called olfactory sensory neurons which are found in a small patch of tissue high inside the nose, these cells are connected direct to brain, there is lot more happening between these two for the smell and from our experience we all know that some smell holds memory or emotion with them. The moment we smell it, our brain immediately shifts to there, like when I smell pancake or hear the word my brain immediately shifts myself to the childhood where my mama is making rice pancake on one winter morning that was the best rice pancake I have ever had.

This smell thing gave me the idea, which I applied in the business. there was a temple two km away from my home, people from different places used to come here to fulfill their wishes, it was a very famous temple in our region. There were seven trees outside of the gate of the temple their base was covered by cement so that visitors can sit and take rest there in their shadow, here in India if you are doing something inside temple premises like if you are sweeping or taking care of shoes of visitors, watering to plants or burning incense sticks for no reason then you are a good man. So, what I did was, every day early in the morning before any visitors come, burn two incense sticks under each of seven trees and I make sure that each stick should that much thick and long that it can run at least two hours so the visitors could smell it.

Another thing I did was meet every shop owner who sells all pooja ingredients give them my loose incense sticks and some money and requested them to give two of my incense sticks to every customer who comes to buy pooja ingredients for free doesn't matter if they want to take another brand you just give them my two incense sticks.

The reason behind that is every person connects emotionally with God. It gets stronger with their faith and believe every time they enter the temple my increase sticks were welcoming them and the two loose sticks in their bucket, they can't throw it because somehow it connects with God. they definitely going to burn it in their home. The idea was somehow if I can able to fit the smell in their mind. whenever they think about their wish, they remind the temple, God and that smell. Whenever they smell the fragrance, they remind the temple, God and that shop where they got free incense sticks. In their mind they have to force themself that, if they want to fulfill their wish. They must please God with this particular fragrance.

This looks completely Hypothetical. You can't Increase your sale like this. This is Insane right? but surprisingly it worked. after someday I changed the fragrance but This time it has a name on it, Rest of the work done by mouth to mouth. The demand for my incense sticks starts to Increase it took pretty good time and lot of my capital to burn this free. Still, I managed to do that because I had nothing to lose. I started all these with zero if something happens I will back to zero and that was ok.

With time we changed fragrance. We collect feedback from our customers and everyone started knowing about us. Later then we promote ourself through celebritys and social media influences and cricketer by the time we learned marketing, managing products distribution. Now we are in the stage where customers buy products with advance payment.

'That was really something not normal', - K said, I have something to clear in my mind. don't you think you Just took advantage of many people's faith.

Look I never said to the customer personally or verbally to buy our product only. Never spread a Rumer that only your wish could be fulfilled if you burn this fragrance only. Never force any single person to take those two incense sticks. In fact, some people have a mindset that why we should take them without paying and some are just throw it and you can't do anything about it. I just took benefit of simple psychology, some perfume science and patience.

Like I said I was not sure about that if this will work or not. I just keep doing about like eight to ten months which was not easy, was it wrong to keep the temple atmosphere pleasant? Was it wrong to give Incense sticks for free? The temple is still there and those seven trees also. every morning our incense sticks are used to start the day.

So, that was the beginning. Now we are making more product along with incense sticks like dhoop, Cones, essential Oils, attars. But Incense stick still our top product till now. It is doing more business as combine other products.

Anything you want to ask?

Nah, I don't have much knowledge about business I just wanted to know the journey.

Ok then wait here, l will bring the car.

No, it's ok, I will Just take a taxi, my training class is not for away from here

You sure?

'Yap, see you in party, this Friday I am not sure but definitely try', Sam said.

'Monson is here, we need special preparation for that', Reema said

Sam is not here, should we start the meeting?

Aunty is not feeling well, He is already managing everything, we can remove some extra burden from him by doing something on our own. In last ten, twelve days the call for snake rescue Increased, no doubt to get warm they enter into private properties and houses. The number of calls are going to increase, we need to prepare for that. Specially in remote areas where is no road. it is mentally frustrating and physical challenge to get there, we need to talk our volunteers prepare for that.

'Lalit, please make the medicine list for street dogs and abounded cow for the disease which is very common in monsoon', Reema said

Finally, Monson is here relief from heat, new season new challenges for street dogs. But nature made them so capable that they can treat themselves on their own and can survive any season, sadly not every one of them are capable for that, Lalit said

The most common disease among the dogs is Kennel cough, popular term for a canine respiratory disease called infectious Tracheobronchitis. There are many possible symptoms for that disease which are sensitive to cold temperature, forcefully coughing with a honking sound is the first and most obvious symptom. For Kennel cough, other like runny nose, watery eyes, sneezing, mild fever also symptoms for that.

It is caused by the Bactria is Bordetella and Best prevention is Bordetella Bacterium vaccine. Other some common diseases are skin infections and fungal infections. This issue cause redness, itching, rashes, hair loss and unpleasant odors.

Ticks and fleas' infections cause significance discomfort and variety of health problem in dogs. These Parasite thrive in moist environment and capable of transmitting diseases such as Lyme ehrlichiosis. Monsoon can contaminate water and increase gastrointestinal problems in dogs that can lead to diarrhea, vomiting, Loss of appetite and dehydration may occur.

All the Issues among street dogs in the Monsoon can be simply eliminated by just arranging a shelter and safe drinking water. Shelter, they can find themselves. No street dog wants to get wet in rain. The problem is safe drinking water. If we can somehow arrange it, this will be quite helpful for them.

While talking about cows' bacteria and other Infections are two times higher in monsoon as compared to other compared to other seasons. The higher moisture content in the air enables harmful microorganism to thrive resulting transmission of number of diseases like Hemorrhagic septicemia, Anthrax, Black Quarter.

Again, shelter is important for them and most of the abounded calf and cow are just in the road and streets. This is tough enough to go through for them. vaccinations are done among our permanent shelter members.

Somesh, please post Monsoon related all the precautions and safety on social media. Make them aware to take care of animals and also themself, mention all the Do's anal Don't with proper eye catching visual and graphics.

On it.

Guys, next two Months are going to be very tough for us, we are on a battle now. But remember one thing we must prepare for the war.

Somesh laughed and said,

Are we in the middle of a play, from where these dialogs are coming from? Is there any kind of setup here?

No, I am serious you are in Odisha, in the Coastal Region. Cyclone and month of August they are made for each other. In every alternate year one cyclone small or big hitting Odisha. We must start our preparation for that. No one knows what kind of destruction it will bring.

Yes, we should start preparing now - Lalit said, although government will provide full support, there shouldn't be any lack from our side.

How is she doctor?

She is fine, it's Just a panic attack, typically it begins suddenly without warning. it can strike anytime while watching TV or middle of eating. sweating trembling or shacking, rapid pounding heart rate, chest pain are some symptoms for this short period of time, Doctor said

There is not any proper cause for the panic attack but the most common reason for that is stress, sense of fear. Though she is absolutely fine now and you can go home but this is alarming. Be with her spend time with her.

How is your business going? and your NGO thing?

Everything just fine doctor, Sam replied

You can take her home now, and take care.

Thank you doctor.

Where is Dr. Mishra? If you have any idea?

Dr. Mishra? visit his cabin once and remember one thing this is alarming, it could lead anywhere, take the best care of her.

I will doctor,

We are still waiting for a donor. If we find today, we can start the process in next day, we tried every close member in his family but not a single member matches the hundred percent accuracy. Now finding a donor for the same is a difficult task on its own, and this organ donation law making it more complicated. Specially Odisha government is very alert in this.

- Dr. Mishra said,

How he is doing? Sam asked.

Amit is a fighter I must say. He is strong and handling it gracefully. The situation he is going through apart from physical pain, its mentally exhausting. I don't know what kind of force pushing him to move forward.

(it's Love - Pony said, It's the future they are seeing with each other, it's such a beautiful thing, isn't it?)

How this process works. How many days we have to wait for the donor - Sam asked curiously,

As I said blood relation members are unable to give their own, we are now completely depending on cadaver waiting list. It could take a month or a year, even if kidneys are available patient must be eligible to get that and it completely depend upon the severity of recipient's kidney condition. Because we are not the only one who are waiting for it. There are hundreds of patients waiting for the same.

I know what are you thinking, pick a rickshaw puller or a daily labor. Throw him money and problem solved, that's not going to happen. There is a Coordinator called transplant Coordinator appointed by Legal Committee of government who closely monitor donor's behavior to bank transaction. They will catch you in seconds.

But there is an argument also, if someone wants to give their organ in freewill for money, which will definitely improve their financial condition or fulfill their needs then it should be allowed by government or not? In this case someone somehow buying the organ which is completely illegal but if someone give their organ as freewill and after somedays receives a plot or some square foot land in his name as gift, both of this thing are look different but it's the same, no matter how strong the laws are there is always a loophole. There is need to reform the human organ transplant act.

What if the waiting stays long? is there any other way to find the donor?

According to transplant act of India for kidney only blood relatives are allowed to donate their kidney near close relationships are also added in past times like grandparents, uncle, aunty other than that no one allows to give their kidney, apart from cadaver list.

Let me tell you a story of one of my patients who was about to transplant kidney but again same situation like Amit then one of his close friends has come to donate his own from Assam as I said there is no such rule for receive from friend too. They knock the court and showed every reason why he wants to give his kidney to his friend then the court came with a term called emotionally related. in some cases, emotional relations are bigger than blood relations that was the only one case specially approved by the court.

'That mean there is still some hope that we can complete this transplant process without depend upon cadaver list', Sam said.

No, No. don't even think about it listen, we have time and Amit doing well, his dialysis going well. The surprise could come in a week or tomorrow.

Or after a year, Sam said

('what the hell he is thinking', J&J said. Is he out of his mind, is he really going donate his own kidney?

I think he is, Gugu said.

Why? for love? Why he is doing this for this stupid thing.

Let him decide for himself. He definitely would have thought about this-Gugu said

Thought? What though? He is going to destroy himself. He won't listen to us. Someone please, stop him.)

There is still hope, you don't have to worry about him Dr. said.

I am not worrying about anything doctor, I just can't see, what he is going through, and the quote "donors live longer", hope this will work for me too.

Are you sure you are going to do this, Dr. asked

You just take care of Amit, I will handle all the legal procedure, even our health minister throwing a grand party and I am Invited. The court thing that also I can handle that much name I have earned.

There will be no difficulty after donation you can back to normal in less than twenty days but listen to me,

This thing what we call our body is a most complicated and sophisticated machine that no one created. it's an evolution process of millions of years that we are living. Your donation of an organ and saving a life is a great thing, but this body is a luxury that we have. It is a legacy we are living without doing anything. We have no rights to tear it apart and stitch it back, no one knows what kind of stages we had gone through to reach here. No one should take it granted.

We can start the per-testing process once approved by the court.

All The Best!

('How are you going to convene the Court? Have you thought about it',
Gugu asked,

I will figure it out,

You will figure it out? It's not a problem in your business, you are
donating an organ, a part of your body, risking your life, you can't say
that - J&J said

I am going to tell the truth, that we are going to get married, this will
make easier.

Are you sure?

'I mean till now you don't have the courage to tell the truth to your
mother, you are going to do it in front of court?', Gugu said with soft
voice

'Look, don't bring the love thing into this matter ok', J&J Said aggressively

Let me ask you a question, did Amit said you, that he loves you clearly?
No,

Then how can you so sure about that. look we are not playing the villain
role like typical Bollywood movie dads who stops two Love birds from
getting married. We just see things more practically- J&J said

'You all are right but for now, my only goal is saving his life', Sam said)

Hey, Mr. philosopher what are you doing here? Party is over
there.

'Hey K,' Lakshya replied.

'I hope I am not Interrupting you guys', K said
What? There is no one here.

The sea is here, the waves are dancing and there must be something is your mind, I mean why would anyone choose to sit here alone in this beach. By the way minister kept his promise. It is one of the grand parties I must say,

Yes, it is, Lakshya replied.

So, what are you thinking?

Nothing, I am leaving next week - Lakshya said, for my psychology PhD.

Psychology? This is something out of mainstream career for society, it's like to choose your own race rather than being part of their race. K said

You also did the same to consider this, we both in same ground but different tracks, Lakshy said

But really you need guts to choose career like that for me it was simple I know where I was best at, but why you went for psychology? If may I ask,

'All credit goes to my parents ', Lakshy said.

I knew it they must have forced your, right?

No, No, it's not like that,

They have given me such freedom that, I can choose my own life and career they have their full support. I know what is in your mind. How much money do I get by taking care of bunch of mental patients. How can I compete with others or society? Lakshy said,

Look, money is never an issue I can spend my entire life without doing anything that much we have. Then talking about competition, I have no competition with anyone at all. I choose it because I always wanted to be on that field. If you see most of the counseling psychologist who take sessions must of them are doing it for free. Why are they doing it for free? Are they don't need money? of course they need but when you are doing something that you really love and passionate about it, that's hits you differently.

It's like when you dance, is there any money thing in your mind? You just do it, flow in it, disappear yourself with music. But at a stage money will definitely follow, we all know that. Mental health still a new topic in India.

According to national health program by the ministry of health and family welfare, close to sixty to seventy million people in India suffer from a minor or major mental disorder. WHO says average suicide rate in India is eleven in every lakh people. Statistics show that one in every five individuals suffer from mental health illness symptom. The age between fifteen to twenty-five is crucial because fifty to seventy-five mental health issues began and developed in between these ages, to resolve that you know what we have, according to some data only one psychiatrist in for every four lakh Indians. We as a society not far behind to contribute it. If someone going through worse mentally and Looking for Psychiatrists, automatically a 'Mad' tag attached to that person. If you are not able to control your mental state, you are weak as a person. No one ready to talk about it, it's like taboo. Even if you expressed about your mental health, The very first thing they will do is laugh at you or they will be in shock when they hear the ward psychology like you do. This ignorance and fear for society leads to suicide.

Another thing is insurance companies don't cover who are admitted in hospital with mental illness. A good treatment doesn't come cheap without insurance cover. They must understand mental health as important as physical health. It will be not easy to cover all the loop holes but there should be some policy to change.

But genuinely, I think all the mental illness things are royal diseases. I mean look at that, all the depression, anxiety, stress things are only happening to those who are more exposed or who has more than enough, who are doing five things at a time and trying to control everything even what is uncontrollable. Who has no control over their emotion I may be wrong but look at the other side of the story. Look at those people who are living, spending their nights in bus stops, stations or elsewhere. Do you really think depression or anxiety thing will hit them? every day they have only one goal how to get food today. The day when they have whole meal for the day, they are happy. If not then they will sleep in hunger and that's ok. They will not complain to anyone. They will not feel low, they will not feel depressed or anything like that. The next day, they again try for food. They may be physically weak for the nutrition. But there is no Issue like mental health in them, while who has everything, they only trap in depression thing. That's why I call it royal disease.

I still remember that farmer from my village where he used to live, you know the condition of farmers in our country. He used to borrow money from my grandfather. Sometimes he returns money on time, sometimes not, it all depends on the Monsoon and the crops. I still remember his face and shiny eyes. I never seen him stressed or sense of worries or tension or anything. There is always smile in his face.

He had three daughter and a boy. This thing is common in villages so as the dowry thing. Still, he managed the marriage of his all three daughters and this is not a small thing especially when you are a farmer still, he managed all that with his limited income, and while look at us, we are get stressed in every small thing like not a call from our favorite person. How to prepare PPT by EOD. I am not saying we should be machines and don't express anything, but see how easily we are choosing to be stressed.

If you compare average teen from, a developed city to any rural area then, you find the suicide rate is high in cities and almost zero in villages. The reason behind that is their society, environment and their parents. Yes, every suicide is a murder I agree, in cities child are more sensitive they can't even take being scolded by parents or teachers. While for a typical village teen it's nothing to them. They will repeat the same mistake without hesitation until their parents' starts beating them but they can take that too easily but they never think about suicide. Another thing village kid are for away from drugs which is another main reason for depression and anxiety among adults. The more expose you are, the more chance that you get spoiled.

I am not with or against anything. I Just want if we control our emotions. It could be easier to live. But that is not easy. That's why we psychologists are here, If I could change a single life then it all worth it.

'So, you are now a psycho-philosopher', K said

(They both laughed)

I have never taken a philosophy class as a subject but I love reading, I am a bookworm to be honest, to be in top two in every class wasn't that difficult for me apart from that I love playing tennis and travelling too. Wherever I go a book stays with me always, doesn't matter which kind, I just love reading more than anything.

That's impressive only few people can do that. I have a question is it true that philosophy took away everything from a person. leave him emotionless with an empty life. I mean I never seen a philosopher in a luxurious car or living a lavish life style. Definitely I am not talking about modern day religion protectors. They have everything, in fact more then everything. In my mind philosopher means away from normal life with growing beard, always lost and trying to figure out something. Is it true you can't live a normal life once you became a philosopher? K asked.

Absolutely wrong, Lakshya replied,

It's not your fault, people have this kind of mindset. We always think in categories like right or wrong, yes or no, this or that. We can't think beyond that, but a wise man can see and think beyond that. They can read in between lines. Why should a thing must be right or wrong why not it has its own perspective? Philosophy takes away nothing from you, in fact it gives you that vision which normal people can't have, it doesn't make your emotionless, with philosophy your thoughts become mature, which mean you have better control over your emotion. You know the best thing is you can't hate anyone or anything, no matter how bad it is to you. That kind of maturity philosophy brings on you.

Isn't all the magical? Just think about it. How could all this have happened? from a single cell to sapiens to homo-sapiens, from where all the philosophy thing started? What was the first thought of that person who choose to think for very first time, was it what is above his head? Why it is so bright that no one can see it? why it is dark after some time? Where is that big round thing above his head gone? or what is that white blue layer follows them wherever they go? from where the water coming from? Is there any kind of water storage upside down which is covered by the white blue layer? After some time, they could have observed the pattern and after that they could have name them. Definitely this must have taken thousands of years to understood things as they are.

When was the first time we started to feel things. Love for others, kindness, compassion, when was the first time when we started to cry. Imagine someone you see every day, one day he sleeps and next day he didn't wake up and you have no idea what death is, after someday it starts to stink then you realize he might never wake up.

Philosophy makes you more curious. It makes you capable that you can arise right questions to argue.

I am not against anything, now imagine, here in India we touch our elders' feet to seek blessing right?

Yes,

Suppose one of your relative and he is around sixty year, who was not very close to your family came to your home and you touched his feet for blessing. Later you got to know that, a molestation allegation on him and next hearing is after someday, in court.

When he visits next time before the hearing date what would you do? will you touch his feet with same respect?

No. of course not no one would do that will keep myself away from him as much as possible,

Now listen, after hearing, court give the judgement that, he is innocent. All the allegation were false and it was planned to ruin his reputation. What would you do now? will you change your mind?

Umm. NO,

Why Not? He is Innocent now. No allegation on him.

I don't know may be a perception or you can say a negative Impression on him will stop me to do that. - K said

Now, think about closely all these, who is right and who is wrong here.

Is it the old man? Is it the tradition or the society who made an allegation on him or your impression about him. It's clear your thought or impression what is hanging between right and wrong. The old man never said that to touch his feet neither he written the rules. It's only your thought that sometimes he is good, sometimes I don't know.

So, tell me K from where these thoughts came from?

It Just came without putting an effort - K said,

Let's make it more interesting.

It that you who thought about it or it's your brain?

 it's me, obviously. no, wait it's my brain.

What type of question this is, me and my brain we both are one.

If you say, 'me' that means you are saying it's your body, right?

Yes,

So, if I hit you then who will feel the pain? It's your body or brain?

My body will,

Why not brain, if they both are one.

If hit you same but this time you are sleeping then who will feel the pain? or if a mosquito bites you, why you don't feel but your brain acts accordingly, if they both are same.

Because that time my body is in completely rest, so I can't feel the pain.

So, you are saying your brain is feeling the pain this time not your body.

(K saw him with confusion and Lakshya laughed)

Ok last and most common one.

Who are you?

I am not going to answer that, you know me, K said

I know you by your name which is given by your parents so, here see my Identity proofs. This is me. -K replied with frustration.

No, that's the picture of your face on a paper my question is who are you?

Can you feel a person sitting beside you, talking with you and you can see that person? K asked,

Yes, I can.

That's me, I hope you get your answer.

K said with a relief.

But sometimes before you said it's your body, aren't you?

My question is still the same, who are you?

You know what l am not playing with you anymore.

I am leaving, K said angrily,

Lakshya laughed,

I just wanted to show you the beauty of philosophy. If someone carry this type of question in his head then how can they stay with normal people. Philosophers are not emotionless people they are just travelers with the question bank. They have no destination but they keep sharing every bit of knowledge on their path.

Your times are up, now answer my questions it's my turn now.

Are you ready?

Yes, Lakshya said

Do God really exit? where he lives what happens after death?

Hey, hey one question at a time please,

There is different answer for same question, depends upon what community you are belong to.

Lakshya chuckled,

Tell me one thing every bird, animals have different species, right? but there is no god for them. We humans has only one species but different god for different group of people. How is that possible? That means God is also discriminate like we human do, which is against the definition how we describe God.

Or, God created the world and stepped back leaving it to run on its own. like a watch maker do. Make a watch, insert battery, set a time and leave it to tick on its own. This concept is called deism in Philosophy, whenever the battery will go down then the watch maker or God will come and do need full. But the question is remaining same god from which religion? or there is another god of gods will come.

Or, we created this god concept according to our convenience and this is still going on,

What are you saying - K shocked, how can even you say about him like that, who created everything for us, we are questioning about him?

Don't freak out, let me just complete it first and by the way it was your question.

You know our evolution process million year long and our cognitive revolution or mental development started nearly about seventy thousand years from now. Then we ourselves in the journey of evolution, we started cultivation, communication, trade and first time in the history of evolution we got full food and starts to save food for the future.

Then magic happened when your stomach is full and enough food for next meal, what would you do? you can sleep peacefully or take rest like animals, when they are full, they don't think about the next meal they just sleep. But we sapiens had a brain which was also in the path of evolution. Then for the very first time in the history of evolution we used our brain's full portion to think and philosophy is only two thousand and six hundred years old as compared to our entire evolution journey. Indian philosophy is much older than that.

They started to think about almost everything like day, night, rain, sun, moon, about the sea, snow, desert. This thinking process was not happening one part of the world, where ever the sapiens are there, around the globe have the similar kind of thoughts because this mental evolution process was happening at some pace around everywhere, they started making stories about every activity they saw like rain, day & night. Remember there was no science out there. Till now if you pick some old religions there is different stories in different religion for the same concept.

They had only one thing to look after is the nature. There were no financial crises, no stock market, then they started respecting the nature and here, the concept of God come from in every old religion around the world, there is separate god for separate element in nature like God of sun, moon, God of rain, God of wind, God of soil and so on.

I am not proofing anything by saying that, I respect every religion and their believe, faith to God, so as their traditions and the rules which protecting them. I am just saying the brain which we have today is a legacy of thousand-year-old revolution process. Why we are believing what others say to us, we invented fire to space station without any help. No god from any religion came to help us on that and never will come.

History is full of blood and wars. Apart from that there was another war going on from the starting of revolution. The war of knowledge, what nobody talks about, in every time period in every part of the world without sword but by using brain. Doesn't matter how you gain knowledge either you support rationalism or empiricism or you are with existentialism, against church or not, just think about it, what if Socrates wouldn't have poisoned. How much knowledge he could have spread. if, Giordano Bruno wouldn't have burned alive in Rome's flower market in 16th century, how much knowledge he could have given to humanity. In India Charwak philosophy stood up against orthodox philosophies. People used to beat them and burn all their researches and papers without knowing what exactly they were trying to say.

We humans never allow, that someone who break our believe system.

In every religion the definition of God is different, so in science, as God particles, you remember large hydrogen collider in Switzerland? where scientists invented Higgs boson and named it God particle. It's not justifying your question but still for some, God is supreme knowledge and for some god is supreme consciousness.

You know what 'K' no matter how hard we try; we can't find the ultimate truth. I mean look at that if God is so kind and give justice to everyone then why a five-year-old girl being touched by anyone who has no existence Infront of God then why God is silent. Why there is sadness around the world? Why there is hunger? Why diseases around the world. Why God bring tsunami?

Now, let's have an argument with that, the war of knowledge that I was talking about. Suppose God created the world, which is peaceful, beautiful and happiness is all around. And there is no place for sadness around the world. No hunger, No poverty nothing. If you got a chance to live there, will you live there?

Of course, why not, K replied

Will you not live there? K asked

No, because that world is also will similar to this world no difference.

How? K asked.

Look, if you can't feel sadness and how would you know the true value of happiness. Where is everyone is a winner then what is the reason left to celebrate. Then there a question will arise who is happier and who is less, alternately there is no difference between these two worlds. I don't know who created this world or it created on its own or by big bang. One thing is clear that, creation is relative not absolute. There is one thing to counter another thing.

I don't know what happens after death but I can assure you that nobody knows the same, though every religion book has a different place after death. Will you go to heaven or hell, you get food, wine or women it all depends on that life you have lived according such books. Our religion thing around thousands year old but nobody came back after death to tell us what happens after death, Isn't it strange?

In recent upcoming five six decades, nobody would find the exact answer for these questions for sure. We still don't know what was before big bang till now. But definitely something or someone is out there which is completely unknown to us. Even if we spend our entire life, we can't find the answer so why not we just live without thinking all this, the limited space and time we have, once it gone never going to come back.

Hope I answered your questions. - Lakshya said

I don't know, but.

I am damn sure this is not the answer I was expecting. Now I am regretting, this was like torture to me.

Uff... let me breath first.

One thing I am very much clear that, I am never ever going to ask any question like that, K said

(again, Lakshya laughed)

Can we just talk like a normal person now?

I am done with this philosophy thing

Yap, sure why not, Lakshya replied

Tell me about your girlfriend, where is she? How she bears all these?

I don't have a girlfriend,

So, you are saying you never been in love?

I didn't say that.

So, you have a girlfriend,

No,

Ugh... Can we just answer like a normal person please, K requested

I am answering it, you are the one who is not listing, being in love and having a girlfriend are two different things. That's what I am trying to say.

When you say I love the rainbow or rain, for that do you need a partner?

No,

You, just love, because you love.

I know exactly what you want to hear. About the relationship. How do you trust each other, how much you love each other, about the biological and chemical thing. But for me that's not only thing about love, to be honest I am not capable to describe the word "love".

That's interesting, I can hear that, say more about it, K said

We all see things differently, feel things differently, but Love is only feeling. That we almost feel like same, mother's love for her child no matter in human animal or bird are same. Something that we can't explain. sadly, in humans love word move around only between two partner or couples. There is not anything wrong about that, but this is only a portion of love. Love as whole is way more beautiful. From ages our poets, writers describe love like that in their Poems, Stories and Ghazals and of course in our Movies also, while the other side of the love is still untouched, very few among us can feel that.

I am not an except and I don't think whatever I am saying everyone should agree with that. For me love is different, it is innate. It is something that we bring with us from the day we born. Later hate and all the negative things taught by the society. The anger, revenge, possessiveness are only showing cruelty of human being is the name of love. When there is love, there is only love and complete freedom, nothing else, nothing to prove, nothing to fight for. For me everything starts with love. Having a friend for every stage of life is love, having is supportive relative and cousin is love someone you know you can't be together wish for him or pray for her is love. Everyone hates Monday still they go to work, crushing their dreams to support their family that is love. That street dog who waits for you for a piece of biscuit that is love. Staying in relationship is love, being single is love, growing old together is love.

You know for me what is purest form of love?

The love without attachment. When you say, I love this or that, when that thing goes away, you become cruel or revenge machine but when you have nothing to love, still you are in love, then you become love. Please understand this, it is very deep. In a certain way you connect with the universe, of course you need certain path and meditation to reach that stage where, there is always peace and joyfulness. when you are extreme happy you start dance right? But body has different mechanism to express purest form of love and it is 'tears' and your chicks should be washed by that tear once in a while, when I say without attachment is the purest form of love at that time you caring love in you but isn't that also something you attach with, when this 'Love' also detached from you then you become beyond love. The universe this sand, this wave, this sound are all become one. But all this 'yogic' thing, we shouldn't go there.

Wow how you know all this? This is beautiful, K said

But tell me one thing will not that be boring?

I mean life is combination of thing anger, love, sad, happiness, victory defeat that what making life interesting. How can someone miss this roller coaster ride and be there in constant stage as you said creation is relative not absolute, K asked

Correct, tell me one thing K, once you start riding a 6.5-liter, 12 cylinder, 759 bhp, 720 NM torque Lamborghini, will you ride any other normal car? you may say yes, but you will not, no one will, once you there in that state of enlightenment all other things become nothing to you. Because all those things are depended upon your emotion. If you don't want to get angry then no one can get you angry once you get over your emotion. There is only joyfulness left.

You are a mechanic also; I didn't know that

At this age every man is, Lakshya replied

Ok one last question, how important money matters in our life or how much money do we need for a happy life.

You don't need any money to be happy, Lakshya replied

As excepted- 'K' Murmured

Just kidding, of course money is important, without money you can't survive in this world money is a parameter which defines a country, state or a human. If you earn respect, honor that will not fill your plate, money will.

Let me tell you a story,

Story about Diogenes one of the famous ancient Greek philosophers in 4ᵗʰ century B.C the craziest philosopher in the history. He was father of 'Cynicism' which is a philosophical thought of school which says relation of conventional desires in favor of simple moderate life.

Again, philosophy I am done with it, K said

No, no we will not go there just listen,

Diogenes has many crazy stories about him. He used to live in streets with no home, no material thing nothing. He used to beg, he had only a wooden cup to drink water when he realized a dog drinking water without cup, then he throw his cup and use this hand to drink water. According to him to be happy only one thing you one need is 'you', the less thing you have the happier you are.

One day Alexander the great came to the city. Diogenes was popular that time for his crazy theories about material possession. when Alexander approached him, Diogenes was sitting in a barrel.

Alexander said, - I am Alexander the great the mighty conquer, whatever you ask for I can grant to you.

You know what Diogenes said.

I am Diogenes the dog and I would like you to move a little to the right, you are blocking my sun.

Alexander was completed shocked with his answer and remain silent for a while. Then he said I am Alexander the great but if I was not, I would like to be Diogenes the dog.

I am not saying everyone should be like him but history is full of such persons who bet everything to find real happiness. everyone should earn money, we as a civilization has to move forward only problem is attachment for that, how down a human can go for money there is no limit.

If you look closely our entire moral ethics and value system is completely depend upon that one bridge. The day the bridge collapse, you will see the real nature of humans.

Let me explain,

How much money do you have right now in your wallet? Whatever it is it's not your whole money that you own. Most of the money that you own is in Bank or in investment form, right? everyone has same. We can say the money more than we need is Just a number in a digital screen, that is your money no doubt, but it is somewhere in cloud storage or in a server. suppose, this internet thing gone mad, for two three days or a simple malware attack on your digital form of money, what will happen. The bridge will collapse and these civilized human beings will tear each other. That day we will see the power of money no god can save us from that, Lakshya said.

'You guys are here? Party is about to start let's go', Sam said.

Hope I am not disturbing you?

Thank God you came, I am about to merge with ocean, you saved me. - K said with relief,

Anyway, welcome to the philosophy club', Sam said.

(Sam and Lakshya both laughed)

Ha... Ha. very funny, K mimicked

It's already seven let's go there, Sam said,

Hey Losers,

Why not you picking the calls, Ravi said.

Eight missed calls, was in silent Lakshya replied, I got something for you guys, and it is my last', Ravi said

'Oh, no why you didn't tell us before that you have Cancer? anyway you will be remembered in our heart forever', Sam said

(everybody chuckled)

Very funny, see no one laughed. I am leaving for Bangalore. Our head chef moving there and he wants me to join him. We are going this Sunday.

Oh, that means you all are leaving.

K are you also? Ravi asked.

Yes, next week to Chandigarh. That's what friend do, they left you when you need them the most', Sam said with a sad voice

But don't worry I will be fine.

Are you going to take this to home? Bring it what you have.

We have Odisha's Signature sweet 'Chenapoda' with some Italian touch with Mascarpone cheese.

And? - Sam asked.

What and? This is it - Ravi replied

Are you not going to share its recipe?

This time not, since the is our last meet, I want all of you to miss this thing like hell.

Oh, in your dream', Sam chuckled.

Ok, as your guys requesting this much, I am going to tell you the Mascarpone cheese recipe.

'Oh, thank lord, for doing this favor to us', K said

(Everybody laughed)

Let me taste it first. You continue, Sam said.

Bring fresh cream, put it in a bowl and simmer the cream and make sure it doesn't boil.

Are you guys even listening to me? why are you eating like you are hungry since a month, you please continue Lakshya said, then add lemon juice, stir at low flame till the cream becomes thick, cool down to room temperature. Then take it to a cotton to refrigerate overnight. Bring it from fridge and your Mascarpone cheese is ready.

This coffee touch is really enhancing the flavor, Lakshya said

Yeah, it's Tiramisu but in desi version it's a combination of Chena Poda and 'Tiramisu' so you can call it 'Podamisu'.

Okay let's go guys, party is about to start.

Wait, can we just sit here for a while?

'No one knows, when will be the next time we will meet like this', K said in slow sad voice.

I want to share you something guys. I am giving my kidney to Amit', Sam said

What?

(Everybody shocked).

Why didn't you wait for a donor?

Already in the list, but no one knows how much time it will take and his condition getting worse.

Does Mama know about this', K asked

No, I will tell her.

When?

That's not the point

Wait, wait, how that's not the point?

She doesn't know you are a gay. She doesn't know about your relationship with Amit and now you are going to do this without telling her anything.

Trust me 'K' I will tell her everything, it's not that easy that you are thinking,

Is it more difficult than giving a kidney?

No, but listen to me I will tell her everything once the complications are over.

What new complication? - Lakshya asked.

He is giving an organ what more complication than that', Ravi said.

According to organ transplant law, both are should be in blood relation or in certified relationship like marriage.

'So, are you going to get married with Amit or what?', Ravi asked

No, we have never talked about it but there is another way of emotional relation, which court will verify and give permission.

How you will convince the court? I will figure this out.

That's why l am here, talked with health minister to forward the process.

If you want, I can stay for a week, Lakshya said

No, no I will manage, I have already consulted with doctor regarding this. It will being normal in six or seven days.

Come here guys, I never imagined, friendship could bring this much pain, K said while sobbing. K are you cleaning your nose in my solder? Sam asked.

Stop, you idoit.

Oh, you are crying that's Ok.

Hey K, what is your story?

Enough for today, maybe next time, when we meet, what if there is no next time? Ravi asked. Then you will remember me forever, some Incomplete stories have best ending.

She is learning too fast,

Hey guys look at the sky,

We all are crying here and someone cerebrates with fire crackers, anyway it's beautiful.

How is the preparation going on? Sam asked.

Everything is going well. It's mid-July and it could probably hit second week of august. That mean we have only twenty to twenty-five days to prepare for everything.

We are in constant touch with govt. of Odisha. Here is the list of shelters that govt. working on it. We could take help of Locals as we can't make our self-present every place during that time. - Reema said

'Hey guys check this article Mr. Jacob broke up with Samul', Somesh said.

What? Mr. Jacob is a gay?

This is not surprising these things are taboo only in India, - Somesh said.

Sometimes I wonder, how do they do things? I mean for us it's simple, one male and one female. Thats it.

'Something called top bottom in their language. I don't know much about it',

Are you guys done?

'We have much more Important things to discuss', Sam said irritatingly.

This is last month data including all the expanse and donation since cyclone in next month, we will prepare the excepted expenses in next two days.

Ok keep work on that we don't have much time.

(Are you going to tell her everything - Gugu asked.

I don't know, may be yes - Sam replied.

Again, in same stage it's like DejaVu or my life in a loop. In every two three months it's like I am back where I started.

It should be ended by the time, look how nice acting he is doing - J&J said. He exactly knows only he can end this thing. Still, he is pretending like innocent.

J&J could you please stop your mouth for a while we all know that it is not easy for him', Gugu said

we can shut our mouth but I can assure you one thing. If this thing will not end today than it will go on forever. J&J said,)

Someone is early today, is everything ok? -Mama asked.

Yes, Mama everything is fine.

You are not looking good.

Everything is fine Mama, how is your leg? Show me.

It's not looking good; I am making an appointment for next month.

Simu, look at me, you want to say something?

No,

I mean yes,

It's ok what happened? Mama asked in a soft voice,

Amit is not doing well, kidney transplant is last option left and we successfully arranged a donor.

That good news, why are you saying this with this expression?

I am going to give my kidney to Amit,

(There is complete silence for one minute)

Please mama say something,

Nothing, as you grown up and you think you can take your own decision without involving me, what can I say, it's not like that Mama, I was scared. how will you react.

Simu, come here, Sit

Don't know why you took that decision. If you think about me yes, I am dying inside in this moment. No mother in this world would allow this, as you already decided to that, make sure the decision shouldn't be completely emotional. Life is better when we take decisions in between.

Remember one thing son, this world is a cruel place, if you think this world will fair to you, l am sorry this is hard but, this is not going to happen. But being good a choice, there no parameter to measure goodness. If you are good then you are good that's it.

Mama kissed his forehead and said whatever you do, I am with you

'Thank you, Mama', Sam said.

Anything else?

Nah, Mama let's have dinner.

('Don't you think, Mama's reaction was obvious like she already knows things', - Gugu asked

I also feel the same, pooh said

How this is possible only my three friends know about this. no way, Dr. Mishra will tell everything, Sam replied

I don't think, she can take these things so easily. how can a mother simply accept it without reacting.

Wait look at this table, isn't it the same plastic container, K had taken 'Gajar ka Halwa' for her parents when she visited last time.

NO, NO, NO this, can't be true.

This means K was here and she already told everything to Mama.

(Sam Run to his mother hugged her and started crying)

I am sorry Mama; I can't even give you this little happiness like other sons. Sam said while sobbing.

Mama also started crying,

No, Simu, lam sorry,

I don't have any idea. You fighting this battel alone for how many years. I should be the one who always supposed to be there by your side not against you. I am sorry for everything.

Here, look at me.

I don't care about this society, this world or anything, only thing matters to me is you and your happiness,

"Thank you K" - Sam said silently.

Dr. Mishra said you want to see me? Sam said,

'Yes, why are you doing this, please don't do this we can find a kidney within time', - Amit said

I am doing this because you need it the most.

And you think you don't need it? Please don't do it. You have done already a lot for me.

I am doing this for us, Sam replied

Just listen to me before you do this and how you going to convene the court?

All the laws and court only there for to make sure there is no illegal transaction of organ or money. They have to make sure someone must not do it for money or not being forced by anyone.

If these two things are clear then others can be taken care. Luckly, I have that money that, I don't have to sell my organ for money that obvious. If I am able to convene the court with this honesty and I am doing it because I only want to save a life then it will be definitely in our favor.

You woke up, here take these medicines. This is Seetal my fiancé, we will be engaged soon.

(What did he said, his fiancé - Gugu said

Yes, he is, Pony said furiously

How can he do this? don't he has a heart', Pooh said

Welcome to the game guys, remember what Mama said days before. This world is a cruel place, J&J said. Then why the hell he kept act like that - Gugu said.)

That one tight slap on your face, when you feel everything just stopped at its place. You know what is happening but you can't act. You stand still like a rock, where everything stops eyes starts to speak and it knows only one language "tears".

Sam... Sam...

Yeah, congratulation both of you.

I know what are you feeling.

No, you can't - Sam replied with teary eyes and a smile.

Sam, sorry for everything, since we spent a lot of time together. I knew you need someone to hold your hands. Unfortunately, I was not that person, and I can't be that one. One thing is very clear is that I admire you a lot. The respect for you still the same trust me I wasn't pretending that I was with you, I was with you but not the way you thought. I don't know how to explain this. It just happened. I had an idea what all this leading to and someday we have to face this together. But I don't have an idea that it will end like this. I can't change things, no matter how many times I say sorry. It's like I am stabbed you while you looking at my eyes with love.

(Sorry only works when you have time machine or you have the power to change things. If not then it's just a word. - J&J said.

I still can't believe that what kind of excuse he is giving, why humans are so cruel - Pony said.

Why they are pretending like God, while they are pure devil inside.

I am always thankful to God that I am not human

You are dead - J&J said

We all are, that doesn't matter, we have to take care of him - Gugu said don't worry about him, He can handle. He has seen worse. J&J said

Pony if you get a chance to be a human for a day what would you do? Pooh asked

I will show them. How to do love without any intention. I will show them someone can be really happy without stealing others happiness.)

'It's ok guys, it's not that for the first time I am facing this. I am fighting the same battle every day and trust me I have seen worse', Sam said

Please don't feel sorry about that, I was not also completely sure about that, I talked with Ravi and Lakshya about this. I was just accepting the situations. I wasn't completely on to you. So, it's nothing to worry about. I am fine.

You know when the very first time my heart completely broken when I was in sixteen or seventeen after my tenth board. My father already left us that time and my mother used to work others home to meet our daily needs, doesn't matter how your conditions are, the hormones and biology thing start their work when you are in a certain age. For the first time I started to feel love and the same butterfly thing in stomach.

There was a boy from different street of my village was one year older than me and tall and handsome as compared to his age group boys. every day he used to come to village ground to play and I was there only to see him. I never participated any game as I was too skinny and my intensions were clear only to see him. I stated to dream about him. You know everything what first love made you to do.

They used to play a game called mud and stick for that they need five or six player more is better. One day they are out of players and they invited me to play. I clearly said no but when he asked me, I immediately said yes. How could I say no, for the first time he talked to me so, I said yes maybe it was the love thing who made me to say yes.

According to the games all player has their sticks and to start the game someone has to show the number of number of players played, in back of one player and he has to guess the name for the numbers, whoever come last will be the victim. The rule was simple everyone has to hold their sticks, except the victim, his stick will be the ground, similar to hockey, players have to drag the ball to the goal post, here we have to drag the victim's stick to the end point with our sticks. Here not game between two teams but victim against all the members. The twist is during dragging you can't rest your stick-on mud or on air you only can rest it in solid things like rock, brick, stone but you can't keep it on air. During the dragging if victim will touch you and your stick not in solid things then your will be next victim and your stick will be dragged end point and it was last of our village and we have to go through streets to reach there and people usually don't give attentions, as it was very common in villages. Another twist is if they successfully dragged victims stick to the end point and he can't make another victim before that then here, He has to drink one sip of dirty water from that pond which was at the village end and come back to starting point by holding his stick in mouth and one leg in air. He must have to cover the distance by jumping in one leg. This game was weird and brutal but in villages it was like that.

In first round he was the victim and we are six players including me and he was so sad, no one wants to be a victim in this game. Seeing him like this I did the stupidest thing, I told them I will be the victim as I am playing for the first time, everyone agreed and smile came back to his face. Game started and everybody was enjoying Including me, my thought was clear this game should go as long as possible. So, I never touched anyone except him while his stick on the rocks. I have to make sure that too. I was pretending That I am in the game but I was in a different game.

We got closer to the end point. Suddenly they started making fun of me, about my body, my face, my father and they started to push me. I don't have any idea why they started all these, maybe they got bored in the game. They started bullying me. This was not part of the game. They crossed the limit when they started making fun of my mother, sad thing was he also doing the same thing with them, I wait for some time still they didn't stop, so at that moment I gathered all my strength and punch one of them so hard that instantly he starts bleeding everybody shocked. Then they started to beat me together, they tore my shirt and start to beat me with their sticks. They dragged me to the pond. They tried to remove my pants, I used my full strength to stop them and begged them not to do this, no one listened to me. I sited on the ground, so that they can't remove it my entire body was full of red lines with stick mark and my face was full of blood. Then they hold my leg and hands lifted in air and he tried to remove my pants, I was crying and begging them not to do this. He couldn't remove the hook so he tore it by force near the chain. They didn't stop there. They lift me in air as much as they could and throw me to the pond, my head hit on a rock and it starting bleeding, after that they left.

I was thinking what was my fault, why they did this to me. I never said to play the game. They requested me, I wasn't the victim, I only did it for him. There was no way I could go home naked in streets' after sometime I decided to end this thing with me. I Just had to find a better way to kill myself. I tried to hold my breath in water but it didn't work. There was no way to find a rope and hang on a tree without clothes. There was only one thing in my mind I had to end this with me. Then I found an old rusty piece of blade. Its sharpness was gone, still it had that much that if I force a bit more then it could cut my veins in hand suddenly a sound come.

Hey,

It was Ravi, I didn't know where he got the news but he come with his clothes.

You may think why he is telling his boring story to us but this is me. The way he brutally killed my feelings about him, it changes my thought about love. so don't worry about me, take rest.

Now I have to leave.

'Let me drop you', Seetal said.

(They both come out from the ward then Seetal said,)

Thank you so much for whatever you are doing. I can feel your heart, what it is going through. I knew about you since Amit joined to your company. I could have stopped Amit, but I didn't, somehow, it's my fault too. I will not say like Amit that don't give Kidney I will never do that because I have to save my love. You may call it selfish; I will call it love, for you I may be the most hated person. But it is clear that Love is a destruction, either you destroy yourself to save your love or destroy others to save your love.

Sam Just give her a smile and left.

Congratulation Mr. Samarendra Barhad, you won the case, court allowed to give your organs I have never seen someone this much happy before donating a kidney. Dr. Mishra said

Seriously, in twenty-three-year career I never seen something like this, even the blood relatives also come with fear and hesitation. Then there is you, are you really a human being?

Let's quickly start the process doctor tell me what are the testes I have to go through, Sam said

Oh, there is a lot it will take weeks.

From starting to your blood group to psychiatrics test, for one reason and one purpose only the person who is donating can live a healthy and happy life after the process. Remember you have to live with one kidney, so we have to make sure that one should function really well.

But before that we have to taste the kidney which you are going to donate, something called kidney function taste, then hemoglobin and blood parameters. Then we have to test your Cardiac, Lungs. Then there is test for your mental health and make sure you are not any kind of pressure in external.

Then something called kidney angiogram for surgeon, who is going to remove your kidney. It is basically the road map for the transplant process to make sure everything will go as per plan.

Then we can start the process, so keep your patience have rest.

Mama, please stop crying, it's just a police case. I can manage all these. There is nothing to worry about.

I don't know why he is doing this to us. We have not done anything wrong to anyone, what he wants from us.

Mama by blaming God, there is nothing going to happen, it's our problem we have to figure this out. Now I have to go to police station.

No,

You can't go with this condition, it's hardly five day's you just donate your kidney you are not completely ok. There is still some swelling in that spot. I can't let you go.

No, Mama, I am ok, remember what doctor said it will go with time, I can do my regular job with medicine I am glad that Amit also doing well though he needs more time to recover. According to doctor it was so accurate like magic, it's not that I am the first person who give his organ there are thousands of donors and they are perfectly fine and doing very good in life.

Ok Mama I have to go now. I will be back soon. Then we will do lunch together.

(Sam left for police station)

Good morning, Officer,

Good morning Mr. Barhad

Is everything ok?

Please sit.

So, there is a complaint against your company from sector three. Three of one family Hospitalized, reason was, when someone burn your incense sticks after two, three minutes, they started to cough and became senseless and then Hospitalized.

That is very unusual Officer, every day thousands use our incense sticks, till now we don't have any issue with that. Apart from that our product is a benchmark for all the government guidelines we have special lab for R & D and testing. There must be something else how can someone Hospitalized by smell of incense sticks even right in the moment, there are thousands of sticks would have burning in different places, are they not effecting by that.

I understand your point, since your company has this much reputation and I know you personally, so I didn't go direct to your company, I call you to come here. Once there is police van in your door step, it will definitely dent your reputation.

Let me read you the full complaint which they are given in written form.

I am Ramakanta Barik age thirty-nine, works in an IT company as server maintenance department. lives in sector three house number six. Got a call from my father Rajaram Barik at nine in morning when my wife and me were in gym. My father told me my mother Ramani Devi, my son Rahul and daughter Rishi found senseless in our pooja room. Then immediately called Ambulance and shift them to Hospital. My father was reading newspaper in garden then he heard a sound of something falling from puja room, he rushed to puja room and found all three on the ground.

Since you run this big company, we have filled FIR and will start investigation soon.

I know Mr. Barhad where this is going, even someone's car has seen around Mr. Ramakant's house. You know what I am talking about. In my career I have seen many such cases, not only in movies in real life this is also happening too. Bring your lawyer, send a legal notice, put a defamation case or do as your lawyer say.

Thank you, officer - Sam said

Please start your Investigation process, as I already told you, we have nothing to fear about, we have our full support. He will definitely drag this matter to court. Hope this will end soon.

Government issued the guideline for Cyclone. It will hit Odisha on August thirteen. Seven days, from now according to meteorological department. It is going to one of the stronger Cyclone about to hit Odisha. Heavy rain fall and the wind speed could reach 130mph. keeping that in mind govt. evacuated 1.2 million people in less than forty-eight hours. Over nine thousand multipurpose shelters were made function overnight where more than 45 thousand volunteers involved. Roughly around 2.6 million text messages are to be sent to locals in clear language before Cyclone hit Odisha.

Regular press briefing done to update people, people are reportedly advised from all source of media not to panic and about Do's and Don'ts before Cyclone, not only govt. But local community groups and volunteer working together. Food packets are making for airdrop by Air Force Helicopters. Senior state officials and police officers are to be sent to the probable effected districts to coordinate, there are 16 NDRF team. 18 units of ODRAF are ready to start immediate rescue operation.

Our preparation also in last stage, so the plan is we start shifting all our wounded dogs and cows to the govt. shelter on 11th august morning. vehicle arrangement has been done, only there is something to fear about is, all the injured animals and human will be under same roof. Let's pray that they will show some humanity to them. we will complete this evacuation process in three trips. In each trip there will a volunteer with them. we have arranged a special vehicle for Radha her child and two dogs Shimu and Sheru as they need special treatment. There will be volunteers for them, we have enough food for two days. Though animal welfare board arranged all the medicine to avoid infection and other diseases - Reema said.

Our website and app are already spreading awareness. There is also a timer in our app which work as a reminder how exact time left that the cyclone hit ground according meteorological department. -Somesh said

That's very good, Sam said.

Here, this is whole data, number of animals we treated, and the exact number in our temporary shelters to be transferred to permanent shelters. We had already given a copy to government.

There is no major health issue among our members except Radha, Simu and Sheru. Other can be shifted normally. - Tusar said

You are doing a fabulous Job guys remember we have to warp this before 12th evening. according to report there will be wind and rain from 13th morning. There will be no power supply, no network, no communication. we have to take care of our family also. Make sure there is no compromise with that. - Sam said

Mama, stop this news channels. They have only one Job to make us alert by giving right information. Instead of doing this, they are spreading fear and chaos all around.

When is your hearing, Mama asked.

It will on 12th, from next day everything will remain closed till further communication. Don't worry about it, Mama, police finished their investigation and they found nothing, it will be in our favor. There is some loss in business but we can manage it. We will find our reputation back once hearing is done. People have so many faiths on us, we will back even stronger.

And what if it will not?

(Sam keep silent for a while)

'It will Mama', Sam said with slow and nervous voice.

Listen son, we are not creator of this world nor the controller of this world, we are not creator of this value system, morals for the society, we humans only think that we control everything, it's not. There is something which controls everything. this jealousy and hate for others are the inner nature of human being. They are just pretending they are good. No matter how good this world will be there is always something bad to counter this goodness. Come here,

Remember one thing Simu.

This world is a cruel place, not because it's not been fair to us but that is its true nature. If you are big and powerful enough then only you get a chance to live here. Same rule for wild animals and humans, and we humane making it worse. There is bad in everywhere. But my son, you always choose good, it doesn't matter if bit more of sadness or suffering comes to your plate. Don't hurt anyone.

It doesn't matter what will the decision of court day after tomorrow, you will choose happiness. Make yourself so strong that, the bad thing may conquer the world but not you.

(Mama kissed his forehead and hugged him)

Let's have dinner together.

(Why it feels like mama knows everything - Gugu said

Every mom knows everything - Pony said

Guys, I don't feel like everything is fine - Sam said

Why, what happened? - J & J asked

I don't know, it feels like something is missing its place.

Guys I am scared, please be with me - Sam said with a crying voice.

We are with you don't worry everybody said.)

12th August the hearing day and the day before cyclone hit Odisha. The judgement to come around 11.40 in morning. That one person in black suit will give a statement which will decide the future of my company or me or my years of hard work or that every drop of my sweat involved in it. A sentence which has the power to charge life.

The question is who give them the power. From starting of our evolution process we tries to find out the difference between good and bad. We are always trying to be good over evil, till now we are not succussed. It doesn't matter if is a Monarchy or democracy there is always a system for justice. But who are giving justice which side they are in? who created these laws, how can they decide what is right or wrong. There is always a battle between good and bad. If something is good for me then why it becomes bad for others in this case whom do you punish. How this justice system will work.

When Eve eat the apple from forbidden tree with Adam, God punished everyone Including serpent. But in our system only humans get punished, nobody talking about the evil, the hate, jealousy and all the negative thoughts. How can we punish them we can only punish someone's body what about their emotion what if they remain same even after punishment? Then this justice system is nothing.

I am only here because of one individual whose evil thought forced him to do a fake case to end the competition. Irrespective of result, we can't change someone. Then the justice system fails here.

The Judgement came and it's a win. may the paper which runs the world did its work or some number in their account or some land in someone's name worked their job perfectly.

Court said all the investigation, report submitted by police is not enough. So, the Court orders to stop the production immediately until a report submitted by a special agency.

Here one thing clear that, no matter how good you are. There is always something out there to control. The evil always wins.

The news is spread all over same speed as Cyclone is coming towards. Few hours left to hit the ground, my phone ring right before leaving court room. It was Raghu. For the very first time in my life, I am this much afraid to take a call my hand is shaking and my heartbeat not in control in those ten second, I have imagined everything that could go wrong, I had no control over my body or emotion. I skipped the call.

Immediately he called again, this time I received it without taking a second. I hear a crying voice; my heart starts to beat faster. He took a second and said,

Mama is no more...

Suddenly my heart beat stopped or it feels like complete silence Inside my body. Raghu was saying something like we are in Hospital, I took mama immediately to the hospital after she called me, she was saying pain in her chest and difficult to breath but before we reach hospital mama stop responding. Then doctor said it was a heart attack.

But by the time my ears stopped responding after that first sentence, he said, I was listening but, I had no sense of words or its meaning, my eyes were seeing everything but it had no sense of visuals. I couldn't speak I couldn't walk; it was like my complete body paralyzed. In my body I was completely dead and, in my mind, it was repeating only one thing 'Mama left me', I had no idea where I was, what am I doing here, what place this was somehow, I gather myself and rushed to hospital.

Everyone has a fear. This fear thing is at its extreme until that thing happened to you, when the thing suddenly happened and you are facing it. The fear is gone along with the thing that you feared for. Death, why is everyone hate this thing? Only reason I found that, it takes away our loved once from us.

Then why the definition changes when our enemy dies, that moment why we can't hate death, we all know it is ultimate truth of life no science till now able to beat death. Since nobody wants to talk about death.

Is the fear of losing someone or the love for someone stop them to think about death, nobody knows what exactly death is how it feels, what happened after that. We only know one thing is, the person we love will never come back to us. everyone has after death stories depend upon which religion you belong to. No matter your burn them or burry them. There is one thing very clear that. There will be Judgement of your Karma's or good deeds, depend upon that, God will decide, your soul will go to heaven or hell. There are different punishments for different religions. No one know what exactly happens, are these only written in religious books or all the things are true. One thing clear that, no religion talks about the person who left alone on earth, who has to live by dying everyday who is missing his loved once. Nobody talks about the pain and suffering that he is going through.

It was an old adage, when a person dies, a universe dies with him. The world he is imagined, his thoughts, his emotion, his opinion, his existence dies with him. We can't save a single thing of that person not his world which existed in his brain, except the memories which exist in our brain only. If we get a chance to bring back our loved once or at least could talk to them like we do in cell phones. How many of us will do that? probably everyone. It will be against the law of nature. We all know that, if something exits permanently without an ending then there will be no love or compassion for that thing. Death is a law of nature if there is no death. There will be no fear of losing someone and there will be no love.

Nature Sometimes cruel but not biased, all the after-death stories in every religion may not true but the fear of punishment of soul, pushes every human to do good Karma. That how it works.

Suddenly phone rang and it took me few seconds to figure out where exactly I am, in last forty-eight hours every thing worse happened to me, that anyone could ever imagine, only one thing is remembered is that my Mama's face before last good bye, then I realized I am in office chair. Then I saw the watch on the wall and a single bulb was glowing in office. It was almost nine at night. It was raining outside and wind picking it's speed. There were only few hours left Cyclone to hit surface.

Again, phone Rang, Luckily the network was still working till that time. There was no power in entire city and only inverter was doing its job in office, I saw the phone it was Reema.

Yes, Reema, Sam said

Is everything ok?

Sorry to disturb with this situation, I am supposed to manage everything but I failed. Reema said while crying.

It's ok please tell me, what happened?

We successfully, shifted all of our members to govt. Shelters including their food for two days but Radha her child, Simu and Sheru are still there

Why? what happened?

The vehicle we arranged for, to shift them has broken down. after two long hour he said the spare part is not available he can't fix it, all this happened in today morning. Then we started to search of another vehicle. It took three hours to find a vehicle but he said no. It was not his fault; people are so scared about the Cyclone that they refused to step outside from their home. We tried to search for another till evening, then one driver agreed, to shift them to government shelter. Surprisingly he didn't charge anything.

Then what is the problem?

It was all planned later we got to know that. That bridge which connects is collapsed due to heavy rain. If he will take another route, it will take four hours to reach there. He wanted to help but said no, after seeing all condition against us.

Still now I am trying to arrange something, praying God for that, l am sorry it was my fault I should have planned for this first, - Reema cried.

Stop crying Reema, I will do something don't worry. So, you are saying that bridge is collapsed so we can't go the government shelters, can't bring them to office it is not safe here, no one know how these strong winds will behave. But I can shift them to my house. It will easier. Anyway, it's just a concrete wall with roof without my Mama.

Reema, you take care yourself; I will do something. we can't let them stay there. All I have to do is reach home before cycle hits. Sam said, how will you do this? Radha can barely stand how can you push her to the deck of the Van? Reema said.

I will figure this out, you just pray that, that old pickup mini truck doesn't betray us. All I have to do is arrange a tarpaulin sheet to cover above its deck so that it can work as a roof, it will save them from getting wet and cover them from wind too. It will work temporary Shelter too. Then find a way to drag her or to push her to the deck, I can't just lift her by hand, but I could do this with Simu and Sheru and Radha's child can walk on her own.

Then I arranged two flat thick woods from our storage area, anyway it will remain closed till the court give permission and rushed to the shelter where they were. Kept that two flat woods with minimum angle to the surface so that Radha can walk to the deck easily. By the time I arranged all this and shift them to deck of the vehicle I almost lost around two hours. Now only less than two or three hours left for the cyclone to hit the surface.

In every minute the rain and speed of wind is increasing only good thing about this truck is all four wheels are doing their job. One of the head light isn't working, door glasses are not working, horn is so slow that I can't even hear it. Though we don't need that there will be no one on the road blow the horn to, water drops are hitting so hard to the front glass that, if I continue drive in this condition, they will definitely break the glass within an hour. I can only see one meter ahead. Though I know the road very well I know every hump every path hole of that road. In normal it only takes ten minutes to cover these three kilometers but, in this condition, it will take not less than one hour. My only fear is there is another bridge one kilometer before home, hope that should be alright. The speed we were going, definitely we are going to meet Cyclone in mid-way.

For the thing I wasn't prepared to happen, it was in front of my eyes. It's like murphy's law worked perfectly. The thing you fear the most likely to happen to you. There was a tree lying on the road, right before that bridge. Now I had no idea if that bridge is ok or not, I can't see beyond that tree. Now I had to go there and check physically that if there enough space to drive the truck or I have to cut some branches to cross it. The moment I tried to open the door. I feel pain on right side of my belly, then I remember some days before, I donated my kidney. I lifted my shirt bit up to see the stitches if everything ok? It was worse and the stitches starting to detach. Ignoring that when I step outside, I can feel the wind in my entire body, I had no idea what is the speed but it was difficult to walk alone on the road without any support, no doubt cyclone was on the ground, and in few minutes, it is going to hit us. According to meteorological department it will cover a huge radius. Luckily major portion of the tree was off the road only top of that tree is on the road which was mostly leaves and small branches. I walked to the Bridge, with every step I can feel that the wind is getting stronger, Bridge condition was ok. There was completely dark everywhere, only you can hear the sound of strong wind, rain and broken tree branches. The plan was clear if accelerate enough with speed I can go through the trees as there were only top part of that tree, mostly leaves.

So, I went back two, three meters accelerated to go through leaves with full speed. In middle of that when entire truck was surrendered by full of leaves and was completely bushy, suddenly the left front wheel stuck in a hole, which I had no Idea that one was there. Since we are in speed, the steering turned left automatically and we are off the road, that was a slope, we were there and within a second all this happened. There was no time for me to react and I had no control over anything, next thing I remember, we are just running down the road with full speed and the front of our truck hit a big rock. That one front light which was working that was also gone. Luckily, we were not in the middle of the slope but on the ground down the road. Somehow that rock saved us, with in all this my head hit in the steering so hard that it starts bleeding. My right side of the body below the chest was completely wet by the blood and my face was also in blood. I have not taken a nap in the last two days nor eaten anything. My body starts to react on that and I felt drowsy and sleepy with pain then I lost my sense there.

When I opened my eyes, it was completely light everywhere, is it next day morning or it was just a dream whatever happened, I had no Idea where I was there was no pain in my body and no sign of kidney transplant stitches. I was like any other normal person. Then it felt like something coming towards me. It's Gugu, Pony, Pooh and J&J all there and running towards me and Pony was so happy that, she was dancing out of Joy and Pooh also.

What you guys doing here? What this place is?

Is this a dream? Are we all in my brain?

Oh, wait am I dead? - Sam asked curiously.

Sam is going to live with us forever, we will play every day, there is no one here to disturb him.

Pony was repeating these lines like rhyme while dancing with Pooh. They both are so happy.

You are right Pony l am going to live with you. I didn't know that this place was so beautiful. I can touch you I can play with you we will be together forever, Sam said full of tears in his eyes.

Honestly there is nothing left for me over there, mom was right this world is cruel. They took everything from me. from the day I born to till now only thing I got is suffering. I can't even revel my true identity or live as I want to be because they're so cultured society is not ready for it. My father who was supposed to save us from everything, he became monster to us, when I tried to get love like everyone else in the world, one beat me to hell, other one took my kidney. I stand a company by putting my everything on it, I wasn't competing with anyone. I was just doing my job, still they locked that, my three friends they also left me when I was in my worst phase of life and guess what, still the world was not satisfied with that, they took my Mama from me, whom I loved the most.

That world can't see me happy even if I go there and find new source of happiness. They will take away that happiness too.

Sam is going to live with us forever...

Will you please shut up your mouth for a second you little rabbit and big fluffy marshmallow, J&J screamed to Pony and Pooh.

Gugu why you silent, do you also want that he will live with us forever, you exactly know what this mean J&J said to Gugu by looking her eyes.

I just want to say, whatever choose l am with him.

Gugu said, lowering her head.

What is wrong with us guys, a happy beautiful life is waiting for him out there, instead of encourage him to live, we are stopping him, what kind of friends we are, J&J said.

How do you know a happy life is waiting for him, all his life he got only suffering, struggle and sadness. Life treated him so brutally that I will pray God that no human should suffer like him. Will you give the assurance that in future he will not suffer again. Pony said to J&J angrily.

No, we can't, no one could. J&J replied back, guys please stop fighting. J&J, I don't have the courage to face the same thing again. l am done with life; l am going to stay here with you guys.

Life was completely unfair to you, we all know that, we are sorry, we can't do anything about that but everything has two sides. All the pain and suffering made you who you are today and look at this place. This is just a memory land, which has no existence in reality.

No one knows how many billions of people had born and gone on earth. No-one remembers them, no one cares, if you dig any square inch of land there might have hundred dead bodies if you equally distribute number of deaths from the revolution. from lord Rama to Jesus to Osho they sacrificed their entire life for the goodness of the world to make this world a better place. Is this the world, that place they have ever imagined? No still they didn't give up their life in between the journey, like you are going to do. Neither Alexander the great not Hitler. No matter what was their principles or ethics. They live their full life until death hugs them. Death is a miracle or surprise from God or universal process no one knows. We just born, grow up, get old and we die, our entire universe work like that, doesn't matter if you are an earthworm or a star waiting for supernova. Everything and everyone have certain time, you are not supposed to break the chain, we all are part of the cosmos and the same law is applying to all. You don't know from where you came from or it's Just a simple biology, no one knows. Every religious people talk about the soul about its immortality, how he changes its body like we change clothes, this, that but no one talking about life.

Tell me one thing If you only have a soul. Is there a single thing you could do with it? Taste, smell, run or anything, but with life you could do anything you want. For us life is the fruit that we all eating which we never paid for, it is a luxury, it's a legacy we have to carry forward.

I can't believe J&J saying all these, Pony said

From where you guys gained this knowledge?

It doesn't matter. Only thing matter is we have to send him back as soon as possible and we can't do it alone; J&J said.

We must not forget Radha, the poor cow her child, Simu, Sheru still out there. What is their fault, we have to save them.

Humans spend their entire life by thinking past or future, while they have life in their hand. The present, they have no control over their thoughts and emotions. If something happened ten years back, they are still suffering for that same as over ninety percent thought in their mind will not come to reality but they still suffer for that. Someone's uncontrolled emotions made you suffer but as I already said before you are not looking other side of the story. It's their fault why you punishing yourself for this. You should first control your emotion "You should make yourself so capable that, all the external things couldn't effect you. You must take charge of your own emotion and thought. It's your life. You should be responsible whatever happens to you.

Just look at the big scenario, hundreds of people hurt you, first thing is you never hurt them back. How many families are smiling because of you and look at your life till now, how many people you helped, how many animals you have saved. For us the definition of being good is who never hurts physically or emotionally, not only humans but animals, trees and environment.

And for us you are a good person. If you give up, the world will lose a good person. The world has only few numbers of good persons and you are one of them.

Emotion is such a beautiful and magical thing that you all humans are blessed with but never bother to use it in a right way. Look at us we are just happy when our stomach is full. We mate in seasons, wag tails when our loved one around us. We can't feel things like human, like success, the feeling of first love, heartbreak. The pain when someone leave us. The happiness when you meet someone after a long time. The sweet jealousy for our loved once, possessiveness, failure and death.

Isn't this emotion making life more interesting and meaningful. Human life is like ride on a tide someone who knows it, they start to enjoy life and who has no attention to life. They live every moment in fear.

The world is a beautiful place. Here everything is beautiful. The flower on the tree, the rain and the Rainbow in the sky, the ocean, sunrise, river, forest, desert, the snow, the moon, the sky full of stars, mountain, beach everything is beautiful, but a human can see its beauties. They have a fully developed body, a brain, and the emotion which shapes everything, we animal, we live there but humans feel everything sometimes I feel jealous that why I am not a human.

No human knows where heaven is, except some texts in every religious book but nobody seen this heaven themselves and surprisingly humans has not any proof that they are not already in heaven. The moment their emotions are sweet the world becomes very beautiful place or heaven. If their emotions are bitter then suddenly this same world becomes hell because humans have given such authority to their emotions that their emotion decide heaven or hell for them.

There is no beautiful thing then life when emotions are in control from the first cry of a newborn baby to last breath of an old man before death. Here everything is beautiful. All human only needs a heart to feel it. Being in love or alone, smile or tears everything is beautiful. Every human says smile and tears are two different things they can't meet. But when they will meet every human could know the true meaning of life. If we were gods then we could have blessed every human that their cheeks should be wash by tears of joy and happiness once a while.

Okay I will live, Sam said while wiping his tears.

(Pony started crying).

Pony, Pooh, look at us. Listen carefully, we all are dead, we only exit in his memory. The moment he decides not to think about us, we are gone, before we are here, we had our own existence J&J the twin squirrel Pony the rabbit, Pooh the white bear and Gugu a dog. We all killed by humans and he tried to save each one of us expect pooh, but he couldn't so, he keeps ourselves alive in his brain or in his memory land. We have no life.

But he has,

Please let him go.

Listen Sam magic will happen when you start to live.

Gugu wiped Sam's tears with her tiny paws and said now you have to leave. They are waiting. They hugged each other and Pooh pushed him.

I opened my eyes with a shock, I had no idea for how much time I was there, some minutes or few hours. The blood flown from my forehead are in my eyes and I can't see properly. I have to wash it; from the wind speed and rain I can guess that we are middle of cyclone. Simu and Sheru continuously howling. That was terrible situation. There was completely darkness all around I had no idea about Radha and her child still alive or not. I touched my right stomach and it felt like about two or three centimeters of flesh already hanging as the stitch detached and from that spot blood was flowing, what I did was bring that old cotton which I used clean the truck and bind around my stomach fully tight so that rain water can't enter to my body through that spot.

The effect of cyclone was at its peak. It was now more difficult to walk around without any support. The very first thing I had to do it was, check them if everything ok or not? When I opened the door and step to the ground it was full of water till my ankle. We were at the river front that river which we were supposed to cross, about twenty meter down the road. Usually, it doesn't get full even if in rain season but this year it was different. Luckily, we were on the surface side where the water flow was slow. I went back to check them, Simu and Sheru stopped their howling by knowing someone is coming, they are alive but I had no way to check Radha and her child with this complete darkness. I can't even ride to the deck of the truck because a little pressure on my stomach can detach the stich completely. Then I tried to listen the sound of her breathing but that also not working with this heavy rain and wind. Then a sound came like hitting metal, maybe she was trying to get up there, it was a relief that she was with us. Whatever I have to do, I have to do it quick. Then suddenly lightning started to make this worse. I can't wait here till the cyclone pass and who knows how much time it would take, even if I wait here, by the increasing flow of water and speed of wind can easily push our truck to any direction and that would be worst way to die.

Then I remember there was an old crematorium as per my Information, it is not in use for two years, a new one replaced in other location. I was there some hours ago with my Mama. It was a hall-like design with cement roof so that everyone can burn their loved once after death even in rain. That place a bit above from the ground and steps are there, if I could shift them to that place then we could survive or at least keep ourselves safe from lightning and massive wind. The problem was with this pitch dark, I had to find out at which direction it was. It's should have fifty meters from here.

I tried to start the truck It had only one head light and that was also gone. The water level was almost to the wheels. Though lightning is scary but I can easily see two meters by that flash of light. The truck didn't start I think I was asking too much to it. Now what I had to do is search that crematorium with this heavy rain and strong wind without any support all alone. Till now the water was up to my knees I have to do this fast my steps are stuck in mud and wind was pushing me back against my direction. I had put on extra effort with each step. After thirty meters walk, I found it. Thanks to the lightning and our evolution process our eyes get adjusted according to the situations.

Then I went back to the truck and now I had a bigger problem. How do I shift them without truck. Without wasting my time and thinking much, I pick up Simu in my arms, keep him close to my chest and bend my neck a bit so that he can't get wet and start walking towards crematorium. With every step it feels like I am closing to death. This time it's not fake, every cell of my body started responding that I am stretching too much. Somehow, I reached there and rested him gently on the ground. I have to leave Simu there so that I can bring other three to that place. I did the same for Sheru. Now Simu and Sheru in crematorium and Radha her child in truck.

Now I can't take Radha and her child to my arms, she is almost a month old. I tried everything to bring her out of truck, I dragged her, pushed her. Honesty my body didn't had that much energy to put an extra effort for her, only she could do it for herself. She was not even trying to shake her leg or maybe she was so frightened by the rain and darkness and every minute water level is rising at that moment when I was completely hopeless, I hear a sound is saying, "maybe it's your destiny, accept it". I climb back to the deck and lie down with her. I just prayed to God that to save Simu and Sheru. we all three can feel that death is near. I Just put my arm around her a neck and closed my eyes.

Then in few second, suddenly I hear a sound when I open my eyes, I Saw Radha was trying to stand up. I immediately placed that flat wood between the truck to the ground so that she can easily come out from the deck and she came out without any support, it was like magic. I walked in front of her and she started to follow me and her child followed her. It's like she is not walking, some divine power doing it for herself. Few minutes in rain, lightning, thunder and heavy wind we finally made to crematorium. Simu and Sheru were so happy that they start to dance by wagging their tails, even their legs are broken and started to licking my face.

I couldn't believe all fours are here, I hugged them. I was so happy that I started clapping and smiling but the more is smiled the more I cried, it was state of complete Joyfulness, its indescribable.

People say, smile and tear can't meet, but right now in this stage I am feeling it. They were wrong. This is the smile and tear, J&J was talking about, its magical when these two meets. "Life is Really Beautiful and I will live till death hugs me".

It has been three months from that night next day morning we all are rescued by ODRAF team. I was in hospital for fifteen days till complete recover. Later I honored with bravery award by various organizations and govt. of Odisha too. Many national and international media covered that story. I have given many interviews for that. For some time, I was social media sensation. This time success or failure doesn't affect me anymore. I have not given that much power to any situation to control over me this simple thing I have learned from life. When you are happy you don't have to tell the reason to the world. In fact, you need absolutely no reason to be happy, happiness is inner nature of human life.

Court given permission to start the production. They didn't find any point against to us and company got one Cr. for the defamation. Amit is handling entire company. In fact, he is getting married to Sheetal in this December. Reema, Tusar, Somesh and Ridhi all doing very well for 'Happie tails. Everything at its place I only miss my Mama a lot.

There is a notification sound disturbed my thoughts. It was from that chat group which was in almost bottom because there was no talk for six-months people only give promises but fails to keep it, it was our chat group me, Lakshya, Ravi and K. They all are coming next month. There was another notification and this time it says. "Mr. Denial Jacob started following you".

J&J was right no one knows the future, no one knows what tomorrow will bring, even if I get a chance to see my future, I will not see it, because I have a most beautiful present. Now it doesn't matter if the world kind to me or cruel to me. I will face it more gracefully with open arms because '' magic will happen when you start living".

www.ingramcontent.com/pod-product-compliance
Lightning Source LLC
Chambersburg PA
CBHW021446150726
47989CB00001B/411